Love

The Legacy of Cain

Studies in Austrian Literature, Culture, and Thought

Translation Series

Leopold von Sacher-Masoch

Love
The Legacy of Cain

Translated and with an Afterword
by
Michael T. O'Pecko

ARIADNE PRESS
Riverside, California

Ariadne Press would like to express its appreciation to the Bundeskanzleramt — Sektion Kunst, Vienna for assistance in publishing this book.

Translated from the German
Das Vermächtniß Kains, Novellen von Sacher-Masoch.
Erster Theil. Die Liebe. Erster Band.
Stuttgart. Verlag der J. G. Cotta'schen Buchhandlung, 1878.

Library of Congress Cataloging-in-Publication Data

Sacher-Masoch, Leopold, Ritter von, 1835-1895
 [Short stories. English Selections]
  Love; The legacy of Cain / Leopold von Sacher-Masoch ; translated and with an afterword by Michael T. O'Pecko.
    p. cm. -- (Studies in Austrian literature, culture and thought. Translation series)
  Four novellas taken from two cycles of novellas entitled Die Liebe and Das Vermächtnis Kains. Contents: The wanderer — Don Juan of Kolomea — The man who re-enlisted — Moonlight.
  ISBN 1-57241-119-8
    1. Sacher-Masoch, Leopold, Ritter von, 1835-1895--translations into English. I. Title: Love; Legacy of Cain. II. O'Pecko, Michael T., 1947- III. Title: Legacy of Cain. IV. Title. V. Series.

PT2461S.3 A26 2003
833'.8--dc21   2002038326

Cover:
Art Director: George McGinnis
Design and Photography: Matthew Richardson

Copyright ©2003
by Ariadne Press
270 Goins Court
Riverside, CA 92507

All rights reserved.
No part of this publication may be reproduced or transmitted in any form or by any means without formal permission.
Printed in the United States of America.
ISBN 1-57241-119-8 (paperback original)

.KUNST

Sacher-Masoch, Leopold Ritter von
1836 - 1895

With the kind permission of the Bildarchiv, Österreichische
Nationalbibliothek, Porträtsammlung

CONTENTS

The Wanderer 1

Don Juan of Kolomea 16

The Man Who Re-Enlisted 69

Moonlight 118

Afterword 181
    Michael T. O'Pecko

The Wanderer

> "Only God knows how long
> this pilgrimage will last."
>
> *Ivan Turgenev*

Lost in thought, our flintlocks on our shoulders, we walked, the old gamekeeper and I, through the primeval forest that lies in heavy, dark masses at the foot of our mountains and that extends its huge limbs far out into the plain. The evening made the seemingly unbounded area of black, virgin conifers appear even darker and more silent than usual; not a living creature's voice could be heard near or far, no sound, not even the rustling of the treetops, and there was no light anywhere in the distance except, from time to time, for the pale, dull golden net that the setting sun spread across the moss and the ferns.

The sky, cloudless and pale blue, became visible only in single patches between the motionless and venerable crowns of the spruces. A heavy scent of damp decay hung in the giant needles and grasses; nothing even snapped under our feet. We walked upon a soft, yielding carpet. Now and then you would see one of those weathered masses of stone, covered with green, that penetrate deep into the woods on the slopes of the Carpathians or even into the grain of the yellow flatland: mute witnesses to that half-forgotten time when a great sea rammed its tides against the jagged coasts of our mountains, and as if it wanted to remind us of those solemn and monotonous days of creation, a strong wind suddenly arose and drove its invisible, rushing waves through the heavy treetops, the trembling green needles, and the thousands and thousands of grasses and shrubs that bowed down humbly before it.

The old gamekeeper stood still, ran his fingers through his white hair, brought into disarray by the wild, streaming winds, and smiled. Above us, an eagle hovered in the blue firmament.

"Do you want to shoot him?" he asked with a drawl.

"How would that be possible?" I asked.

"The storm will drive him down," the old man murmured without changing his stance. The black, winged spot over our heads did, indeed, grow larger from second to second, and I could already see the shine of his feathers. We were approaching a clearing bordered by the somber spruce, among which single white birch trees stood like skeletons in an anatomical museum, and red rowan-berries glowed here and there.

The eagle circled calmly above us.

"Shoot now."

"You go ahead and shoot him, old man."

The gamekeeper half closed his eyes, squinted for a while, then took his rusty rifle from his shoulder and cocked the trigger.

"Should I really?"

"Of course. I wouldn't hit him anyway."

"Then in God's name."

The old man calmly laid the rifle against his cheek, a flash of light flew upwards, and the forest echoed the shot with a rumble.

The bird flapped its wings and seemed to be carried upwards by the air for a moment longer. Then it fell to earth like a rock.

We hurried over.

"Cain! Cain!" Suddenly from the brush, there rang out a voice as stern and mighty as that of the Lord when he spoke to the first people in paradise or to the cursed man who had spilled his brother's blood.

And the branches parted.

Before us appeared a creature of superhuman wildness and strangeness.

A man stood commandingly in the bushes, an old man with gigantic limbs, bare-headed, with flowing white hair and a streaming white beard, and large, dark, threatening eyes, which he trained on us like a judge or an avenger would. His hair-shirt was torn and patched in several places, and a drinking gourd hung from his shoulder. He leaned on his pilgrim's staff and nodded his head sadly. Then he stepped into the clearing, lifted up the dead eagle, whose warm blood dripped onto his fingers, and studied it silently.

The gamekeeper made the sign of the cross.

"He's a wanderer,"[1] he whispered with bated breath, "a holy man."

And with that he quietly hung his rifle on his shoulder and disappeared between the century-old, brown trees.

Against my will my foot had become rooted to the ground, and I was almost compelled to study the eerie old man.

I had often enough heard of this strange sect to which he belonged and which stands in such great veneration among our people. Now I could satisfy my curiosity.

"What have you profited by this, Cain?" the wanderer turned to me and said after some time had passed. "Is your murderous lust stilled; are you satiated with the blood of your brother?"

"Isn't the eagle a predator?" I quickly replied. "Doesn't it murder the smaller and weaker members of its race? Isn't it more of a good work to kill him?"

"Yes, it is a murderer," the peculiar old man sighed. "It spills blood like all creatures that live, but must we therefore do the same? I don't murder, but you—yes—yes—you are of the race of Cain. I know you; you have the mark."

"And you," I asked in embarrassment, "who are you, then?"

"A wanderer."

"What is that?"

"Someone who is fleeing from life."

"Strange!"

"Strange, but it is the truth," the old man muttered. He laid the dead eagle gently upon the earth and looked at me with some sympathy, and suddenly his eyes were infinitely gentle and comforting.

"Look inside yourself," he continued with a trembling and admonitory voice. "Reject the inheritance of Cain, recognize the truth, learn renunciation, learn to despise life and love death."

"How can I follow truth if I don't recognize it? Teach me."

"I'm no saint," he replied. "How should I teach you the truth? But I will tell you what I know."

He took a few steps toward a rotting tree trunk that was lying on the floor of the forest clearing and sat down on it. I sat not far from him on a mossy rock. He rested his venerable head in both hands and stared off in front of him, and I let my arms sink onto my legs and prepared to listen to him.

"I am also one of Cain's sons," he began, "a descendant of those who ate from the tree of life, and I must make amends for that and wander—wander until I'm free from life. I've also lived and foolishly taken pleasure in my existence and surrounded myself with trumpery. I too have done that. I called everything mine that a man can acquire with his constantly unsatisfied desires, and I have learned what their worth is. I have loved and been laughed at and trampled under foot when I loved with all my heart. And I've been worshiped when I wantonly toyed with other people's feelings and the happiness of strangers, worshiped like a God! I have discovered that the soul that I thought kindred to mine and the body that my love considered sacred were sold like goods in the most despicable trading. I have seen the wife entrusted to me by the church and the state, the mother of my children, lying in the arms of a stranger. I was the slave of woman and the master of woman and was like King Solomon, who loved many women. I grew up in abundance and had no knowledge of need and people's misery, but overnight the wealth of our house vanished, and when the time came to bury my father, there was barely money enough for his coffin. I spent years fighting for my existence, came to know worry and care and hunger and sleepless nights and fear and sickness. I fought my brothers for the sake of possessions and advantages. I've betrayed and been betrayed, robbed and been robbed. I've taken other people's lives and have myself been near to death. All for the sake of this devilish gold and property. I've passionately loved the state whose citizen I am and the people whose language I speak, and I've been given offices and honors and sworn an oath to the flag of my country. I've marched off to war with angry enthusiasm and have hated and persecuted and killed others simply because they spoke another language. I have harvested nothing but shame for my love and contempt and scorn for my enthusiasm.

"Also like the children of Cain, I have understood how to live at the expense of others, from the sweat of my brothers, whom I have degraded into being my slaves and my tools, and I have not hesitated to pay for my pleasures and entertainments with the blood of strangers. But I have worn the yoke more than once, felt the whip, labored for others, and have striven tirelessly for profit; I have worked ceaselessly from morning until night, and in the night's anxious dreams, I have continued to add up my numbers; and day and night, in good fortune and in bad, in need and in abundance, I have feared only one thing: death. I trembled before it, have spilled tears at the thought of being separated from this beloved existence, and have cursed the whole of creation at the thought of my demise. Oh, I suffered horrible fear and terrible torments as long as I still had hope.

"But insight came over me. I saw the war among the living—I saw human life as it is—and saw the world as it is."

The old man's white head nodded up and down and was lost in thought.

"And what insight came to you?" I said after a while.

"The first great insight," he continued, "is that you poor, foolish people live in the delusion that God in his wisdom, goodness, and omnipotence created this world as good as possible and placed in it a moral order, and that he who is evil and does evil disturbs this order and this good world and that this evil man will be delivered up to both temporal and eternal justice. A sad, fateful error! The truth is that this world is bad and deficient and that existence is a kind of penance, a painful test, a sad pilgrimage, and everything that lives, lives from death, from the exploitation of others!"

"So your insight tells you that man is only a beast?"

"Indeed! The most rational, bloodthirsty, and cruel of the beasts. No other is as inventive in robbing and enslaving its brothers, and so, no matter where you look, in the human race as in nature, there is the struggle for existence, life at the expense of others, murder, theft, robbery, betrayal, and slavery. The woman enslaves the man, the children their parents, the rich man the poor man, the state its citizens. All toil, all fear is only for this existence, which has no other purpose than itself. Life! Life! Everyone wants it. Just keep your life going and reproduce your unholy existence in others. And the second great insight—but you won't understand me, Cain."

"Perhaps I will."

The old man looked at me with pity.

"The second truth is," he continued with a gentle earnestness, "that pleasure is not something real, nothing in and of itself, just a release from gnawing need and from the suffering that need creates, and yet each and every being runs after pleasure and happiness, and in the end, he's done nothing but mark his time until the end of his days, whether he ends in wealth or poverty. But believe me, our misery lies not in renunciation, but only in this always vigilant hope for a happiness that never comes, that never can come. And what is this happiness, that always appears near and within our grasp and yet eternally distant and unreachable, from the cradle to the grave? Answer me if you can."

I shook my head and found no answer.

"What is happiness," the old man continued. "I've searched for it in women, in property, in my people, everywhere where life and breath hold sway—and I saw myself cheated and made a fool of everywhere.

"Happiness? Perhaps it's the peace that we seek in vain here where there is nothing but the struggle whose culmination is the death that we fear so much. Happiness! Who has not searched for it in love above all else, and who hasn't suffered the most bitter disappointments there? Who hasn't been ensnared in the delusion that the satisfaction of the superhuman yearning that consumes him, that the possession of the woman he loves must bring him perfect fulfillment, nameless bliss, and who hasn't finally had a sad laugh at the joys he'd imagined. It is a shameful insight for us that nature has placed this yearning in us only to make of us its blind, willing tools, for what does it care about us? It wants to propagate the race! When we've done carrying out nature's intention, provided for the immortality of the race, we can go to ruin, and nature has equipped woman with so much charm only so that she can force us to put on her yoke and say to us: 'Work for me and my children.'

"Love is the war of the sexes in which each struggles to subjugate the other, to make the other into a slave, a beast of burden, for men and women are enemies by nature, like all living things, united in sweet lust, as it were, united into a single being for a short time by their desires, by the drive to propagate themselves, only to ignite an even more terrible enmity and to battle even more violently and more ruthlessly for dominance. Have you ever seen greater hatred than between people who were once united in love? Have you anywhere found more cruelty and less mercy than between man and woman?

"You are blind, mad fools! You've created an everlasting bond between man and woman as if you were capable of changing nature, capable, with your ideas and fantasies, of commanding the plant to bloom and never to wither or bear fruit."

The old wanderer smiled, and in his sunny smile there lay neither malice nor disdain nor mockery, nothing but the clarity of understanding.

"I have also come to know the curse," he continued, "that is to be found in property, in all forms of ownership. Born of theft and murder, robbery and deceit, it goads us on and creates hatred and fights, theft and murder, robbery and deceit forever and without end. As if the grain standing in the field, the fruit on the tree, the milk of the animals weren't there for everyone. But there is in the children of Cain a demonic lust for property, a cruelty that seizes everything within its reach, if only to prevent others from acquiring it. And it's not enough that the individual uses violence and tricks to lay claim to possessions from which hundreds or even thousands could live; it is as if everyone wanted to set himself up for eternity, himself and his brood, and so he leaves it all to his children and grandchildren who void their filth on silk cushions while the children of those who have nothing go miserably to their ruin. One man seeks to acquire, and the other seeks to keep hold of what he has. The unpropertied man wages war against the property owner, a struggle without end; one rises and the other falls and begins to climb upwards all over again. And there is never compromise or justice. Every day Joseph is sold by his brothers; every day Cain spills his brothers' blood, and it cries out to heaven against him."

As if defending himself, the old man stretched his arms out in front of himself in solemn outrage.

"But the individual is too weak to wage war against his innumerable brothers," he continued, "and so the children of Cain have united into communities, nations, and states for the sake of plunder and murder. It is true that in these groups the egoism of the individual is restricted in many ways, his larcenous and murderous lust hindered, but the same codes of law that are supposed to prevent new crimes lend, at the same time, new dignity to the criminals of earlier peoples and times. And in the state, it is not just egoism that is subject to coercion. Depending on the goals that those who govern pursue, we have forced upon us another's religion, another's language, another's convictions, or ours is at least suppressed and then withers; we are made useful for purposes that we despise, and we are blocked in our own strivings; our sweat, even our blood is minted into money in order to pay for the caprices of those who rule the state, whether these caprices be called luxury and opulence, hunting and women, soldiers, sciences or the arts. Nothing is sacred; contracts of all kinds are entered into and broken without reason or shame. How often has the future of an entire nation been sacrificed to a prince's momentary temptation! Spies sneak into families and dissolve all the bonds of morality and the soul; the wife sells out her husband, the son his father, and the friend betrays his friend. Justice becomes false, and the education of the people, the only means of a general reform, is given pitiful alms, and so knowledge and insight are restricted to narrow circles. Those who represent the people with their words and their pens are persecuted, laden with chains, exterminated or bribed and made into apostles of the lie. Those, however, who serve the state seek only their own advantage under the cover of its cloak and even rob it, though they call it their god, and in the end they repay the nation for its servitude, its shame, and its stultification with bankruptcy. And if the people in their despair transform the tools of peace into weapons against their oppressors, the revolt—whether it ends in victory or defeat—only unleashes the passions and the bestiality of the masses, answering blood with blood and pillage with pillage. Is that which is so highly praised to us as love for the nation and for the fatherland anything else but egoism?

"Nations and states are big people, and like the little ones, they are eager for plunder and thirsty for blood. It's true—whoever doesn't want to do harm to life—can't live. Nature has forced us all to rely on the death of others in order to live. But as soon as the right to exploit lower organisms is permitted by necessity, by the drive for self-preservation, it's not just restricted to man harnessing animals to the plow or killing them; it's the stronger exploiting the weaker, the more talented the less talented, the stronger white race the colored races, the more capable, more educated, or, by virtue of a benevolent fate, more developed peoples the less developed.

"And that, in fact, is the way it is.

"That which would be punished by prison or the scaffold in civil society is practiced by a nation, is done by one state to another, without anyone seeing crime or depravity in the matter. They murder each other wholesale for land and possessions, and one nation attempts to take advantage of the other, to subjugate and enslave it, to exploit or exterminate it, like one person does to another.

"What is war—to which the nation's best march off, seduced by dishonest pretenses and a deceitful enthusiasm—what is war but the struggle for existence written large, the rape of countries and the murder of peoples accompanied by the slavery of service to the flag, espionage, betrayal, arson, sexual coercion, and plunder followed by epidemics and famine!

"Don't we see the same cursed drive at work here in millions? The same drive that in the individual is constantly busy undermining the whole of human existence?"

The old man was quiet for some time.

"Shall I reveal to you," he asked then with solemn composure, "the great secret of existence?"

"Tell me."

"The secret is that everyone wants to live off others, by theft and murder, and they should live off themselves, by means of their own work. Work alone frees us from all misery. As long as everyone strives to have others work for them, to enjoy without effort the fruit of others' efforts, as long as one portion of humanity is forced to suffer slavery and need so that others can indulge themselves in luxury, there will be no peace on earth.

"Work is the tribute we pay to life: whoever wishes to live and enjoy life must work. And everything that fortune grants us can be found in our work and striving. Only by means of a manly, courageous struggle for existence can one triumph. Anyone who doesn't work and who takes pleasure in that condition is, in the end, the one who has been deceived, for he is troubled by that gnawing dissatisfaction that is most at home in the palaces of the fashionable and the rich, a deep disgust with life combined with the most harrowing fear of death.

"Yes! It is death that frightens into compromise all those who are dissatisfied, all who are unhappy, and even most of those who have recognized the essence of our existence—death with its cruelly tormenting companions, doubt and fear.

"Almost no one thinks of the time, wants to think of the endless time when he did not yet exist. Everyone trembles in the face of that second infinity in which he shall no longer be. Why should we fear that which we once were, and were for so long, a state that we became so familiar with, whereas our current condition only makes us anxious by its brevity and besets us with a thousand cruel mysteries.

"Death is everywhere around us. We can encounter it in the moment of birth or later, suddenly, violently or after long suffering and illness or in a massive, general die-off, and yet everyone constantly plans and strives to avoid it, to extend his existence, which sooner or later must end just as miserably, even absurdly.

"How few people understand that it is death alone that brings us complete salvation, freedom, and peace. How few, despairing of life, have the courage to seek out death calmly and voluntarily. It is better, of course, never to have been born, but if one has been born, then one should experience the dream calmly, with a smile of contempt for its shimmering, deceptive images so that one can sink into the lap of nature forever."

The old man placed his brown, weathered hands over his

deeply, sadly wrinkled face and seemed to be dreaming to himself.
"You have told me what insights you have gained into life," I then said to him. "Won't you also speak to me about the eternal truths that you have derived from them, about the teachings that you follow?"

"I saw the truth," the old man cried, "and saw that happiness lies only in understanding, and saw that it would be better for this race of Cain to die out. I saw that it is better for a man to go to his ruin than to work, and I said: I will no longer spill the blood of my brothers and no longer rob them, and I abandoned my house and my wife and took up the wanderer's staff. Satan[2] rules the world, and so it is a sin to take part in a church or a religious service or the activities of the state. And marriage is also a mortal sin.

"And these six things: love, property, the state, war, work, and death, are the legacy of Cain, who slew his brother and whose brother's blood cried out to heaven, and the Lord spake to Cain: 'You shall be cursed upon the earth and a fugitive and a vagabond.'

"The just man demands nothing of this accursed legacy, nothing of the sons and the daughters of Cain. The just man has no home; he flees from the world and men; he must wander, wander, wander."

"How long?" I asked. I was startled by my own voice.

"How long? Who knows," the old man replied. "And when his friend, death, approaches him, he must await him calmly under the open sky, in the field, or in the forest so that he may die as he lived—in flight.

"It seemed to me this evening that he was at my side, solemn, friendly, and consoling, but he passed me by. Therefore shall I take up my staff and follow him, and I will find him."

The wanderer did rise and take up his staff.

"The first thing is to flee life," he said, and an all-merciful goodness gleamed in his eyes, "and the other thing of importance is to wish death and to seek it." And he lifted his staff and continued his wandering. In a short time, the brush had concealed him.

I remained alone in the deep solitude of the forest, and night fell around me.

Before me lay a decaying tree trunk. Its rotten wood began to glow, and a most restless and active world of plants, mosses, and insects became visible in it.

I became lost in thought. The day's images rushed past me like waves or bubbles that the water casts forth and devours again. I saw them without care or fear, but also without joy.

I began to grasp the meaning of creation. I saw that death and life were not so much enemies as friendly comrades, not opposites that negate each other, but rather as variations of nature, each flowing out of the other. I felt myself detached from the world. Death no longer seemed terrible to me; indeed, it appeared less so than life. And the more I became submerged in myself, the more everything about me became alive and expressive and touched my soul.

Trees, bushes, grasses, even the stones and the earth stretched their arms out toward me.

"Are you trying to escape us, you fool? Give up; you can't. You are like us, and we are like you. Your pulse beats only in time to the pulse of nature. You must be born, grow, and decay like us; live, die, and in death give new life; that is your fate, child of the sun. Don't try to defend yourself against it, for it won't help."

A deep, solemn rustling passed through the forest, and above me, the eternal flames burned calmly and sublimely.

And it seemed to me as if I were standing before the dark, silent, eternally creating and devouring goddess, and she began to speak to me:

"You try to stand before me as a being complete in himself, you sad fool! Does a wave glistening in the moonlight become arrogant because it shimmers with greater life for a moment? One wave is like another. They all come from me and return to me. Learn to be humble in the company of your brothers, patient and meek. If your day seems longer to you than that of a fly that lives only for one day, it is only a moment in me who has no beginning and no end.

"Son of Cain! You must live! You must kill in order to live and kill when you no longer wish to live, for only the murder of the self can free you.

"Learn, therefore, to submit to my stern laws. Do not hesitate to steal and to murder like all my children. Understand that you are a slave, an animal that must live under the yoke, that you must eat your bread in the sweat of your brow. Overcome this childish fear of death, these shivers that grip you in my presence.

"I am your mother, as eternal, endless, and immutable as you yourself are limited by space, a victim of time, mortal, and changeable.

"I am the truth; I am the life. I know nothing of your fear, and your life or death means nothing to me. Don't consider me cruel for leaving your life, that which you consider to be your true essence, at the mercy of chance, like that of your brothers. You—like all the others, you all come from me and return to me, sooner or later.

"Why should I prevent it or protect you from it or mourn you? You are a part of me, and I am in you. That for which you tremble is but a fleeting shadow that I cast. Your true essence cannot perish through your death, just as it did not originate with your birth.

"Look to your brothers, how they wrap themselves in their cocoons in the fall, concerned only with bedding their eggs safely, with no care for themselves, all of them going calmly off to die so that they may awake again to a new life in the spring.

"Look into the drop of water, where in the midday brightness of the sun, a new world comes into being every day and perishes in the dusk.

"Don't you yourself awaken to new life after a short death every day and tremble at the prospect of the final sleep?

"Autumn after autumn, I watch with indifference as the leaves fall; I see wars, epidemics, every great die-off of my children, for every one of them lives on in new beings, and so I am alive in death, eternal and immortal in decay.

"Understand me, and you will no longer fear me, nor will you accuse me, your mother.

"You will flee from life to me, to my womb, from which you arose for a short period of torment. You will again return to the infinity that existed before you and that will continue after you, whereas time limits and consumes your existence."

Thus she spoke to me.

And then there was nothing again except a deep, sad silence about me. It was as if nature had compassionately retreated back into herself and left me to the thoughts that she could not liberate me from.

I saw how sacred lies have blinded us, how we, the inheritors of Cain, were not placed above nature as her masters, but on the contrary are the slaves that she uses for her undecipherable purposes and that she has infected us with this anxiety to live and propagate so that she may be certain of their exhausting labors, their oppressive serfdom, their hopeless servitude.

A nameless shiver gripped me and goaded me to tear myself away from her, to flee from her. I pulled myself together and headed toward the open countryside. Thoughts, fears, and doubts flew silently and in shadows about me like bats. And so I rushed down into the plain, which lay there peacefully in the gentle illumination of the night sky and its innumerable lights. In the distance, I saw my village and the friendly, shimmering lights of my house. A deep calm came over me, and in me burned solemn and still a sacred yearning for knowledge and truth, and when I came upon the familiar path between the meadows and the fields, there suddenly stood a great star in the heavens, big and bright, and it seemed to me that it was leading me on, as it once did the three kings who sought the light of the world.

NOTES

1. The "wanderers" constitute the most peculiar and fantastic of all old-believing sects of the Russian Church and belong to its priestly class. In their belief, the entire moral structure of the world has been dissolved, the devil has been installed as ruler over the world, and any participation in the life of the church or the state is pure devil worship, which the pious must avoid by means of flight and endless wandering. Even the acceptance of a passport is a serious sin, for that is seen as accepting the dominion of this world. The wanderer takes no wife and has no property. He does not recognize the authority of the state or the church. He will spill no blood and will therefore accept no military service. The just are

never allowed to have a home; flight from the world is their calling, the only means for saving their soul. Those who do not yet have the strength to break completely with the realm of the Evil One are allowed "for the sake of their weakness" to temporarily hold a job and to take up a permanent residence; but they are required to set up secret chambers where the wanderers can at any time find lodging and asylum. When the hour of death approaches, however, every just man must be carried out into the open field or into the woods so he can be considered as having died while in flight. The sect enjoys great respect among the common people. The eerie figure of the wanderer, who considers himself to be a monk, who rejects marriage as a mortal sin, and who permits only a free "cohabitation of the sexes," is a truly national figure in the great Slavic world of the East. They appear frequently enough in the villages and cities of this far-flung realm and, by virtue of their wildness, the make an inextinguishable impression on anyone who has ever seen them.

2. Satan, whom our people only very rarely call by name, has nothing in common with the cynical German devil, appearing instead as a pure and magnificent personification of the evil (sensual) principle, as the successor of the "black god" in whose opposition to the "white god" the pagan slaves conceived the world.

Don Juan of Kolomea

All the wisdom of my life
Teaches me just this
Do not hope that love will last:
It's fleeting as a kiss.

Faithfulness is but a joke.
Others change like fashion.
If you change yourself, my friend,
Don't expect compassion.

Hymen's trap therefore avoid.
Spouses are maltreated.
Love and cheat on all of them,
Else it's you who's cheated.

Karamzin

We left the district capital of Kolomea[1] and rode into the countryside. It was a Friday evening. The Poles say, "Friday is a good start," but my German colonist from Mariahilf[2] claimed that Friday was an unlucky day, for our Lord had died on the cross that day and founded Christianity.

This time the German was right, for we were stopped by a peasant patrol half an hour out of Kolomea.

"Stop–your passport!"

We stopped. But the passport ! My papers were, of course, in order but no one had thought about my Swabian[3] driver. He sat on his coach-box as if passports had yet to be invented, snapped his whip, and put fresh tobacco in his pipe. He, of course, could be one of the conspirators. His shamelessly contented face was a challenge to my Russian[4] peasants. He had no passport—that was right; so they shrugged their shoulders—that was just as right.

"A conspirator," they whispered.

"But friends, consider! " All in vain.

"A conspirator!"

My Swabian fidgeted with embarrassment on his seat and abused the Russian language to no avail. The peasant patrol[5] knew its duty. Who would dare to offer them a bribe? Not me. So we were gathered up and taken a few hundred yards to the nearest tavern.

From a distance there seemed to be flashes of light from time to time in front of the building. It was a home-made scythe held by a peasant standing guard at the door, and just above the tavern's chimney hung the moon, looking down at the peasant and his scythe. It peered through the small window of the tavern and scattered its light like silver coins, annoying the close-fisted Jew by filling the puddles in front of the house with silver. I'm referring to the innkeeper, who met us at the door and vividly expressed his pleasure at such well-heeled guests by emitting a kind of monotonous wail.

He waddled back and forth like a duck, kissed a grease spot first on my right sleeve, then, for the sake of symmetry, on the left, and cursed the peasants the whole while for "arresting such a gentleman"—he couldn't find a more telling characteristic for me than "such a"—a gentleman who's as patriotic as the Kaiser's black and yellow flag, whose very face looked black and yellow, whose soul was completely black and yellow, he'd "swear it on the Torah." He acted and fussed as if they had inflicted the worst insult possible on him.

During all this I left my Swabian with the horses—the peasants were guarding him—and saved my black and yellow soul by letting it stretch out on the wooden bench that surrounded the large oven in the taproom.

I was soon bored, for friend Moschku[6] had his hands full with serving his guests with brandy and gossip, and only seldom did he hop over the bar to my table, sink his verbal claws into me, and attempt a learned conversation about politics and literature.

I was bored even without that and looked around the room.

Its basic color was green.

The frugally trimmed petroleum lamp filled the room with greenish light. Green mold lay on the walls, the great rectangular oven was lacquered green, and green moss grew out of Israel's fieldstone floor. Green sediment in the schnaps glasses, green oxidation on the small tin measuring glasses that the peasants drank out of when they walked up and put their copper coins down on the bar. A green vegetation covered the cheese that Moschku placed in front of me, and his wife was sitting behind the oven in a yellow nightgown with big bluish green flowers and rocking her pale green child. Green in the Jew's careworn face, green around his small, restless eyes, around his thin, motionless nostrils, and in the mockingly twisted, sour corners of his mouth.

There are faces that turn green with time—there really are—and my host had one.

The bar stood between me and his guests. They were all sitting around a long, narrow table, mostly farmers from the area; they talked quietly among themselves and put their shaggy, ponderous green heads together. One seemed to be the church singer. He was doing most of the talking, had a big tobacco can that he alone snuffed from in order to maintain the necessary respect, and read aloud from a green, half-decayed Russian newspaper.

Everything was quiet, serious, and dignified, and outside, the peasants were singing a melancholy song whose melody seemed to come from a great distance. The notes floated around the tavern like ghosts, and it seemed as if they were afraid to come inside and join the living, whispering people. Melancholy flowed in through all the cracks in the form of decay, moonlight, and music.

My boredom also turned into melancholy, the melancholy that is so peculiar to us Little Russians, a manly yielding to the feeling of necessity. And my boredom was as necessary as sleep and death.

The church singer had just gotten to the obituaries, arrivals, engagements, and train schedules in his green newspaper when the snapping of whips, the clatter of horses's hoofs, and human voices suddenly arose in a confused burst outside.

Then it was quiet.

Then you could hear the voice of a stranger mixing with those of the peasant patrol. It was a man's voice, laughing. It had music in it, but a cheerful, brazen, high-spirited music that wasn't afraid of the people in the tavern. It came closer and closer until the stranger stepped across the threshold.

I straightened up, but I could only see his tall, slender figure, for he was entering the tavern backwards while still joking with the peasants.

"But friends, just do me the favor of recognizing me! Am I an emissary of the Polish revolt? Look at me! Does the Polish national government ride the imperial highway with four horses and no passport? Does the national government go around with a pipe in its mouth like I do? Brothers, do me a favor and be sensible!"

A couple of peasant heads and an equal number of hands then became visible, followed by an equal number of hands rubbing the chins of these heads, which was meant to say, "We won't be doing you this favor, brother."

"Really not ? Do me a favor and be reasonable—"
"Impossible."

"Am I a Pole ? Do you want my parents to spin in their graves at the Russian cemetery in Czernelica? Didn't my ancestors fight with the Cossack Bohdan Chmielnicki[7] against the Poles? In how many battles? At Pilavce, Korsun, Bato, at the yellow waters; they besieged Zbaraz with him, leaving the Poles to lie, stand, or sit as they pleased. Just do me a favor and let me go."

"Impossible."

"Not even if my great grandfather besieged Lemberg with *Hetman* Dorozenko? I'm telling you, the heads of Polish noblemen were cheaper than pears during that campaign, but—let me go and wish me well."

"Impossible."
"Impossible! Really?"
"Really."

"Well then, goodbye." The stranger yielded in a manly fashion to necessity, without complaint. He entered, his face still turned away from me, responded to the Jew's duck-like nods, and sat down at the bar, his back toward me.

The Jew's wife straightened up, looked at him, put the sleeping child on the oven, and walked up to the bar. She was beautiful when Moschku first brought her home—I'd bet on that. But now everything in her face was so unpleasantly sharp. Pain, humiliation, whippings, and kicks had burrowed their way into her people's features for so long that they took on this incandescently wilted, wistfully contemptuous, humbly vengeful expression. She bent her high back, her fine, transparent hands played with the brandy measure, and her eyes locked onto the stranger. A glowing, yearning soul rose out of those big, dark, voluptuous eyes like a vampire out of the grave of a rotting human nature, and it clung to the stranger's handsome face.

It really was a handsome face, and like the moon, it leaned over the bar to her, but it tossed real silver coins onto the table and asked for a bottle of wine.

"Get out!" said the Jew to his wife.

She bent down even lower and left with closed eyes, like a sleepwalker; Moschku whispered across the table to me: "He's a dangerous man, a dangerous man," and shook his cautious little head with the thick little sidelocks.

That caught the stranger's attention. He quickly turned around, saw me, stood up, tore his round sheepskin cap from his head, and begged my pardon in the most courteous manner. We exchanged greetings. Russian affability has embodied itself so strongly in both language and customs that an individual simply can't compete with the tender flattery of social convention. But nonetheless, we greeted each other with more gallantry than is usual.

After we had each described ourselves as the most miserable of servants and fallen at each other's feet[8] innumerable times, the dangerous man took a seat across from me and asked my permission to fill his pipe. The peasants were smoking, the church singer was smoking, even the oven was smoking, but he asked, and I agreed to everything "in order to be merciful." So he filled his long Turkish pipe.

"These peasants," he said good-humoredly. "Me of all people! —Judge for yourself. Would you do such a thing to me and take me for a Pole even at a distance of a hundred paces?"

"Certainly not."

"So you do see, my dear brother!" he added in overflowing gratitude. But try to talk with them." He pulled a piece of flint from his pouch, put a small piece of tinder on it, and struck it on his knife.

"Well, but the Jew says you're a dangerous man."

"Yes, I see." He stared down at the table and smiled. "My Moschku means—dangerous for the women. Did you see how he sent his wife out! These things catch on fire so easily."

The tinder caught on fire as well. He put it in the pipe and soon enveloped us in thick blue smoke. He had modestly cast his eyes downward and just kept smiling.

I had time to observe him.

He was apparently an estate owner for he was very well dressed; his tobacco pouch richly embroidered, his manner aristocratic; either from the vicinity or at least from somewhere in the Kolomea district—for the Jew knew him. A Russian, he had said right away, and he wasn't talkative enough to be considered a Pole. He was a man the women could like. He had no trace of that awkward strength, of that raw clumsiness that other nations consider manly. He was noble through and through, slender and handsome. And yet, his every movement bespoke his elastic energy and his indomitable toughness. His simple brown hair and the short, somewhat curly beard, cast their shadows upon a face that was browned by the outdoors, but well-formed.

He was no longer quite so young, but he had a boy's cheerful blue eyes. Inextinguishable, benevolent love for his fellow man lay lightly on his dark countenance, dark in so many lines that life had deeply cut into it.

He stood up and walked around the room a few times. With the wide legs of his pants tucked into his creased yellow boots, his torso belted with a colorful sash under an open, flowing jacket, and his fur cap on his head, he looked like one of the old, wise, courageous boyars[9] who sat in council with Vladimir and Yaroslav and rode into battle with Igor and Roman.[10]

I could certainly believe that he was capable of being dangerous to women, and as he paced back and forth and smiled, it was a pleasure even for me to watch him. The Jew's wife came back with the bottle of wine and crouched down behind the oven, her eye unblinkingly trained on him. My boyar came over to the table, looked at the bottle of wine, and seemed to expect something.

"A bottle of tokay," he said, "is the best substitute for a woman's hot blood."

He rubbed his chest with the palm of his hand; it gave me the impression that something was burning in his heart.

"I'm sure you have"–I was afraid of being indiscreet, but he quickly completed my thought: "A rendezvous! Of course!" He half closed his eyes, puffed a thick cloud of smoke out of his pipe, and nodded. "A rendezvous. You understand. And what a rendezvous. I'm lucky with women, you know, quite extraordinarily lucky. If they'd let me get my hands on the holy women and the virgins in heaven, I'd turn heaven into—one of those houses. God forgive me the sin! Please believe me—I'm telling the truth."

"I certainly do believe you."

"As the proverb says, 'What you won't tell your wife or your best friend, you'll tell the stranger on the road.' Open the bottle, Moschku, and bring us two glasses—please be so kind as to drink the tokay with me and listen to my amorous adventures, delicious adventures, as rare as a manuscript by Goliath the Philistine, for the silver pieces that Judas Iscariot received for betraying our Lord are not rare at all. Believe me, I've seen so many of them in the churches of Galicia and Russia that it seems he didn't get such a bad deal. Hey, Moschku!"

The innkeeper hopped on over, made a few jerky bows, pulled a corkscrew out of his pocket, knocked the sealing wax off it, blew on it, and finally put the bottle between his skinny legs and pulled the cork out while distorting his face with terrible grimaces. Then, for no good reason, he blew into the bottle and poured the yellow tokay into the cleanest two glasses that Israel tolerated. The stranger raised his glass to me.

"To your health."

He really meant it, for he emptied the large glass in one gulp. He wasn't a drinker—he had tasted the wine too little for that, hadn't taken it on his tongue and brushed it against his palate.

The Jew watched him and said shyly, "It's an honor that so great a benefactor should once again look in on us, and he looks so good, still fit as a fiddle!" While making this comment, Moschku tried to assume the stance of a lion, and he seemed to find it necessary to stretch out his weak arms like the handles of a broken Pompeian jug and to stamp up and down with his feet as if on a treadmill.

"And how is the health of our benefactor's gracious lady and dear children?"

"Good, good!" My boyar poured himself a second glass and drank it to the bottom, but with his eyes cast down as if ashamed. And when the Jew had been gone a long time, he bashfully looked over at me and was quite red-faced. He was silent for a long time, staring off into the distance and smoking. Then he poured a glass for me and said very quietly, "I must look quite foolish in your eyes. You must be thinking that the old ass has a wife and children at home and wants to entertain me with his fantasies of trysts and love letters. Please, don't say anything, I know what you're thinking. But you see, first of all, it's a pleasant obligation to entertain a stranger, and then I thought—once again—forgive me—it's really quite odd. People meet and may never see each other again. You'd think it didn't matter what someone like that thought of me. But that's not true in my case. I don't want to make myself look better than I am. A man becomes a seducer half from lust and half from vanity. If people didn't know anything about my adventures, I'd be the unhappiest man in the world, and so I tell them to everyone, and they all envy me, but today I've made myself ridiculous."

I made some objection.

"Don't bother. That's the way it is, ridiculous, because you don't know my story. The whole district knows what happened to me, but you don't. And then you become so ridiculously vain when women like you, ridiculously vain. You want everyone to think highly of you, and you give away your money to the beggars on the street and your stories to the strangers in the roadside taverns. It's truly ridiculous. But now I have to tell you the whole thing. Do me the kindness of listening to me. I don't know why I feel such trust toward you."

I thanked him.

"Well then. So what else can we do! There aren't any playing cards here! So I guess I'll—but no!—and yet—Consider this—'a good bird doesn't foul its own nest,'—every one of our peasants says that. But I'm no good bird. I'm a high-flying bird, a funny bird. Another bottle of tokay, Moschku! —Let me tell you my story."

He thought for a while, his head resting in his hands. It was quiet. The disturbing song of the peasant patrol could be heard again, sometimes like a lament for the dead from a far distance and sometimes soft and close as if the soul of the strange man were resonating in the desperate, heart-breakingly sweet melody.

"So you're married," I finally asked.

"Yes."

"Happily?"

He laughed. The laughter sounded as harmless as that of a child, but it made me shiver. I don't know why.

"Happily?" he said. "I don't know what to say. Please do me the favor of thinking about what that is: Happiness! Do you run an estate?"

"No."

"But you do understand something about agriculture! Certainly. Well, you see, happiness, so to speak, isn't like a village or an estate that belongs to you, but more like a lease. Please understand what I'm saying, a lease. If you try to set yourself up there for once and for all, if you let the land lie fallow according to the rules or even fertilize or spare the forest or take care of the young trees or build a street," he grasped his head as if in despair—"Dear God! —you're acting as if you had to take care of your children. But what it's really about is getting as much out of it as you can in a year, or even today, not tomorrow. You need to exhaust the field, devastate the forest, ruin the pastures, let the grass grow on the paths, the barns, and when everything has finally been run into the ground and the stalls could collapse at any time—you couldn't do better! Couldn't do better! You enjoyed the use of it, you were as happy as you could be. That's what happiness is! Funny! Funny!"

The new bottle of tokay was uncorked and he poured out a few generous glasses.

"What is happiness!" he cried. "The breath of air that I take. There, you see!" He exhaled. "There you have it! You see! Do you see it?" He pointed with his finger. "Where is it now! A moment, a second on the clock, eventually the hand of the clock ticks—and it's gone! The song that the patrol is singing! Listen to the last swelling note, how it rises and flies and just floats in the air. You'd think it would never end. It carries us away, away—always away! There—there, the night has swallowed it—forever—that's happiness."

We were both silent for some time.

Finally he said, rather cheerfully, "Forgive me for asking, but why are all marriages unhappy! Or at least most of them! What objection would you make to that statement?"

"Me! None, none at all!"

"So you see, it's a fact. But a man who accepts what is without thinking about it or struggling against it is a weak man in every respect. —I think you have to bear whatever is necessary, whatever is fated or is a part of nature, like winter, or night, or death. But is it also necessary that marriages be so unhappy as a rule? Is there—you understand me—a necessity, a rule, if I may so express myself, a law in nature?"

My man posed his questions with the zeal of a scholar explaining his subject. He was apparently sure of his topic and was watching me in a manner that was not the least bit serious, but with a charming curiosity.

"What makes most marriages unhappy?" he repeated. "Do you understand me, brother?"

I said the sort of thing one usually says.

He interrupted me, apologized, and continued.

"Forgive me, but you got that out of German books. That's the way it is. You like to read, I can see that. I do, too, but you get such ideas, such phrases—well I'm sure you understand me. —I could also say, 'My wife wasn't enough for me,' or 'She didn't understand me,' and 'It's so awful when no one understands you.' I could tell you how I'm such a unique person, a real original, how

I have such unique ideas and such completely unique feelings, and how disappointed I am, and how I can't find a woman who understands me, but I'll keep looking—phrases like that, you know—but that's all a lie, all a lie! In fact, my good man, have you noticed that, in fact, every man is a liar! There are only two classes of liars, and you can put people into one or the other. There are those who lie to other people; they're the materialists you read about in books. And then there are the idealists, as the Germans call them—they deceive themselves."

I admit the man was beginning to interest me more and more.

He drank another glass of tokay and really got into the swim of things. His eyes were swimming, his tongue was swimming, and his words truly began to flow.

"Well, Sir, what makes marriage so unhappy," he asked and laid his hands on my shoulders as if he wanted to press me against his heart. "Just think, sir, it's children."

I was surprised.

"But my dear friend," I said. "Take a look at this Jew, how miserably he and his wife live. Wouldn't they run from each other like dogs if there weren't children and love for the children?"

He eagerly nodded his head and raised the palms of his hands toward me as if he wanted to bless me. "That's true, brother, that's true! That's just it—that alone! Listen to my story.

"As a boy, I was, what should I say, a fool. I was afraid of women. When I was riding a horse, I was a man. Or I'd take my rifle and walk through the field into the woods or the mountains—I'm not going to tell you any of my hunting anecdotes—anyway, when I ran into a bear, I'd let him come really close and I'd just say: 'Quick, brother!' He'd stand up, so close that I could feel his breath, and I'd shoot him, right in the white patch on his chest. But when I saw a woman, I got out of the way. If she'd talk to me, I'd turn red, stutter—such a fool, you know. I still thought a woman only had longer hair than we do and longer clothes, and that was all. Such a fool. You know how people are around here. Not even the servants talk about these matters. You grow up, and you almost have a beard already, and you don't know why your heart is beating when you see a woman like that. Such a fool, I'm telling you.

"I thought I'd discovered America or at least a new planet when I finally knew. Just think—children aren't pulled out of the water like crabs. Good. Then I fell in love all of a sudden. I don't know how myself. But I'm boring you, surely?"

"No, please—"

"Good. I fell in love. My late father, God bless him, had this idea to have us learn to dance, my sister and me. So a little Frenchman came with his fiddle and the estate owners came from around the vicinity with their sons and daughters. It made for a happy party of neighbors. Everyone knew everyone else and was in a good mood; I was the only one whose whole body trembled. But my little Frenchman didn't think about that. He put the couples together as his fancy dictated, caught me by the sleeve and also caught a young lady from the neighbors', a child, I tell you. She was still tripping over her dress and had blond braids down to here.

"So there we stood and she was holding my hand—because I—you would have thought I was dead. So we danced. But I didn't even look at her. Our hands just burned in each other's hands. Until at the end, when they say: "Messieurs!" You walk up to your lady, click your heels, let your head fall onto your chest as it if had been hacked off, hold your arm crooked, take her by the fingertips and kiss her hand. The blood shot up into my head. She made the best curtsey and when I raised my head, she was all red and had eyes—what eyes!"

He closed his eyes and leaned back.

"'Bravo, Messieurs!' I was saved. From then on, I didn't dance with her anymore.

"She was the daughter of one of the neighbors. Beautiful! —What can I say. Beautiful! So refined is what I'd say. Every week there was a dance class. I didn't even speak with her, but when she danced the Cossack,[11] her arm delicately pressing against her side, my eyes just bored into her, and then she'd look at me. I'd whistle and turn on my heel. The other young gentlemen licked their fingers like sugar, sprained their hands and feet trying to catch her handkerchief, but she would toss her braids back and look at me.

"When she left, I felt like a hero if I lit the way down the stairs and stood at the bottom. She'd wrap herself up comfortably, give a friendly nod to everyone so that envy burned in the pit of my stomach, and when the sleigh-bells tinkled in the distance I'd still be standing there holding my candle in my hand, so crooked that the wax would drip terribly. Such a fool, I'm telling you.

"Then the dance lessons ended, and I didn't see her for a long time.

"I woke up one night and had been crying and didn't know why. I learned love poems by heart and recited them whenever I could, always to my clothes-rack. I'd have courage then and imagination. I'd take my guitar and sing, and our old hunting dog would crawl out from under the oven and raise his muzzle to the skies and howl.

"Then in the spring, I got the idea to go hunting. I wandered around the forest and lay down above a ravine, and as I was lying there, the branches broke and through the thicket came a big bear, slowly, quite slowly. I was completely quiet, and it was quiet in the forest. Only a raven was flying over me and crying. Then I was gripped by a nameless fear, I made the sign of the cross and didn't even breathe, and when he was all the way down—I ran as fast as I could.

"Then there was the fair. Forgive me, I'm telling you everything in the most miserably confused way. So I go to the fair, and when I get there, she's there too. Oh, right, I've forgotten to say what her name was: Nikolaya Senkov. She had a way of walking like a princess, and her braids no longer hung down, but rather lay on her head like a golden ring, and her way of walking was so free, she swayed, and the folds of her dress rustled so charmingly that you could fall in love with the rustling alone. The fair is really noisy. The buying and selling on all sides, the peasants are running around in their heavy boots, the Jews are darting through the crowds, people are shouting and crying and laughing, and the boys have bought little wooden whistles and they're whistling. But she saw me right away.

"So I get my courage up, look around me, and think: 'Stop! Give her the sun! She'll like that! What more can you give her?'

Sorry, it was a sun made of gingerbread, bright as gold, I'm telling you. I noticed it from far away and made an astonished face, like our pastor when he's expected to bury someone free of charge. Well, this time I have courage like the devil. I go, throw down my twenty—it was my only one—and buy the sun. Then I march on over and just grab my young lady by one of the folds on her dress. That was really quite indecent, but that's the way you are when you're in love, quite indecent! I grabbed her and presented her with the sun. And what do you think my Nikolaya did?"

"She probably said thanks."

"Said thanks! She—she laughed in my face. He father laughed too, and her mother, her sisters and cousins, all the Senkovs laughed! I felt like the time at the ravine when the bear was coming slowly toward me. They're rich people, and we were just—we got along. So I stuck my hands in my pockets and said: 'That's not nice, Pana Nikolaya, to laugh like that. My father gave me nothing for the fair but the twenty, and I threw it away on you like a prince throwing away twenty villages. So please be so gracious as to—' I couldn't say anything more. Hot tears stung my eyes. Such a complete fool, I'm telling you. But Pana Nikolaya took my sun like this with both hands and pressed it to her breast and looked at me. Her eyes were so big, so wide open—the whole world didn't seem as big to me—and so deep! They just pulled you in, and she asked me, with her eyes she asked me, her lips were trembling—

"I began to shout! 'Oh, what a fool I am, Pana Nikolaya! If I could, I'd tear the sun out of the sky, God's own, bright sun, and I'd lay it at your feet. Go ahead and laugh at me, go ahead.' Just then a Polish count drove up. His coach was drawn by six horses, and he was sitting on the coachman's box with a whip in his hand, just flying along, I'm telling you, right through the middle of the fair. It was crazy to drive so fast in a place like that. People started to scream, and a Jew doubled up on the ground, my Senkovs fled—only Nikolaya stood motionless and raised her hand against the horses. I grabbed her around the waist and carried her away. Nikolaya's hands were around my neck. Everybody's screaming, but I felt like dancing with her in my arms. Then the count and his coach were gone, the girl was no longer in my arms. What a moment, I'm telling you. A Polack like that! Driving so fast!

"But I'm telling you everything as I experienced it. I'll cut it short."

"No, no! We Russians like to tell stories and we like to hear them. Keep going like you have been." I stretched out on my bench. He stuffed his pipe with tobacco again.

"It really doesn't matter," he said. "We're under arrest and there's nothing we can do about it, so you might as well hear the story all the way to the end.

"The Polish count had separated us from her brave family. My Senkovs had been scattered to the four winds. Do you think I went looking for them? Pana Nikolaya put her arm through mine, quite gently, and I led her back to her family, that is, I kept looking around so that I could discover them from a distance and turn off into another row of booths before they saw us. I raised my head as proudly as a Cossack, and we chatted. What about? Well, we saw a woman sitting there selling watering cans. Pana Nikolaya claimed that clay is best material for the cans, and I said wood, just to keep talking; she praised French books, and I praised German; she liked dogs, and I liked cats, and I contradicted her only to hear her talk, so charming. And when she got angry—her voice!—like music, I'm telling you! Finally the Senkovs had trapped me like a wild animal, it couldn't be avoided any longer, and we ran right into the arms of Father Senkov. He wanted to go home right away. Good. I had screwed up my courage by now, shouted orders at the coachman, and told him which way to go. First I lifted Madame Senkov into the coach, then I pushed Father Senkov in from behind—you know—all so that I could let myself down on one knee, Nikolaya could put her foot on the other and hop into the coach. Then there are still the sisters and cousins, I kiss another half-dozen hands, the coachman whips the horses, and they're gone.

"It's really—I'm sorry—if only I could—it's such a bad habit—telling stories like this. But it would be better if I just went on, otherwise I'll hold things back. We are, after all, under arrest.

"So, the fair.

"I sold myself there, I'm telling you, me, myself, just like you see me now. I walked around like an animal that had lost its master. I was quite lost.

"The next day I rode out to the Senkovs' village and was well received. Nikolaya was more serious than usual and let her little head droop a bit. I became sad as well. I looked at her and thought, 'Why are you like that? I'm yours, your thing, your creature, do with me what you will, I'm yours, go ahead and laugh!' I really didn't think that she could wish for anything more.

"I started riding out to the Senkovs' often.

"Once I said to Nikolaya: 'Permit me to stop lying.' She looked at me in surprise. 'Are you lying?' — 'I tell you I'm your slave, my soul belongs to you, I fall at your feet, I kiss your footprints, and I'm not and I don't. Permit me to stop lying.' Believe me, I—I stopped lying that very hour.

Some time later our old Cossack said to the servants: 'Our young master has become pious—he has a real shiny spot on the knees of his pants.' Well, now I have to tell you about the dog.

"The Senkovs' village was closer to the mountains than ours. They had numerous sheep outdoors to pasture, near the deep forest. The camp was surrounded by a sturdy fence. The shepherds made their fires there at night. They had their iron-tipped staffs, they even had an old duck-shooter with a barrel and a couple of wolfhounds. All that, as I said, because they were so close to the mountains, and the wolves and bears ran around there like chickens, and there were so many of them, and they reproduced as fast as the Jews.

"They had a black wolfhound.

"They called him 'Coal.'

"He really was black as coal, and his eyes sparked like coal.

"He was the special friend of my—I'm sorry—what am I saying—"

He blushed a bit and lowered his gaze.

"Coal was the special friend of Pana Nikolaya. When she was just a little tot, lying in the warm sand, Coal came along—nothing but a pup himself—and licked her all over her face with his tongue, and the little girl put her fingers between his big teeth and laughed, and the dog laughed too.

"Then the two of them grew up. Coal became big and strong like a bear. Nikolaya couldn't quite keep up, but they still loved one another. And when Coal came to the sheep, it wasn't because they sent him there. Do you understand that? He was so generous by nature that he always had to have something to protect. There wasn't an animal like him around for miles.

"If he tore a dog apart with his teeth, it was because it had bitten another animal. Wolves avoided him and bears stayed away when he was on guard.

"So my Coal got into the habit of protecting the sheep. They were such poor, scared creatures, just right for my Coal. So he joined them and from then on only visited the manor house, and when he'd come back, the lambs would flock around him and greet him, and he'd lick them right and left with his red tongue as if he wanted to say: 'It's all right! I know.' Well, Nikolaya was now making visits to the flock as well, and they both were quite particular. When the child stayed away, the dog sulked, and once, instead of running to the house, he went off into the forest where he had fun seducing the wolf's wife.

"It was a majestic animal. When Nikolaya would come, he'd herd the little lambs over to her. She'd sit on his back, and he'd carry her so lightly—not lightly, proudly!—he knew what he was carrying.

"When I got to know Coal, he was old, had bad teeth; one leg was lame; he slept often, and every now and then a lamb would be lost.

"Around this time people in the area were talking a lot about a bear, a monstrous bear I'm telling you, that had also been seen near the Senkovs'.

"I immediately thought about my bear in the ravine and was a little ashamed.

"Once I was riding over to the Senkovs' when I ran into a group of peasants rushing toward their flock. It was quite a tumult. I spurred my horse on, and from a distance I could hear them crying 'the bear! the bear!' I got scared and galloped over to them, jumped off my horse, and a bunch of people were standing here. Nikolaya was lying on the ground, the wolfhound in her arms, and sobbing. The people were just standing around and whispering.

"The bear had been there and grabbed a lamb. The shepherds and the dogs didn't move. The just shouted and howled for all they were worth. The mistress began to scream, and Coal, embarrassed, jumped over the fence with his lame leg and ran straight at the bear.

"His teeth were no longer sharp. He attacked the bear, the bear attacked him. The shepherds ran out with their flintlock, the bear fled, the lamb was saved, but Coal just was able to drag himself a few feet and he fell, like a hero, I'm telling you. Nikolaya threw herself on the ground by him and pressed him to her breast. Her tears flowed down onto his head; he looked up at her, took one last breath, and it was over.

"I felt as if I had committed murder. 'Leave him alone, Pana Nikolaya,' I said. But she lifted her tear-filled eyes up to me and said, 'You're a hard man, Demetrius,'—that's my name, you see. 'I'm a hard man—is that what you think?'

"I gave my horse to the shepherds, took a long knife, sharpened it a little better, took the old flintlock, pulled out the charge, and loaded it again myself, put another handful of powder and lead shot in my sack and headed off—into the mountains.

"I know that he'd come through the ravine."

"The bear?"

"That's right. I was waiting for him. I stood in the ravine. There was no escape. The walls were so steep and as hard as stone. Trees grew up above, but none of them let its roots so far down that you could reach them with your hand and swing yourself up.

"He couldn't escape—and he wouldn't turn around—neither could I.

"So I stood there and waited for him.

"Have you ever been lonely?—Do you know what that means, to wait for somebody? That's painful enough to tear a man apart, and here I was standing in the lonely forest, and it was a bear I was waiting for.

"A strange caution and the brute intelligence of excitement! I stuck the loading stick into the barrel of my gun one more time to be sure that the bullet was seated firmly.

"I don't know how long I waited.

"It felt lonely, infinitely lonely.

"Then the leaves rustled high above me in the ravine, one step after another, like the heavy boots of a peasant.

"He was just grunting away to himself.

"And there he was.

"He looked at me and stopped.

"I came one step closer to him and pulled—what am I saying—wanted to pull the trigger. I fumbled around and didn't find it—the flintlock didn't have a trigger. I made the sign of the cross, tossed off my jacket, wrapped it around my left arm—and the bear was already coming at me.

"'Hey, brother,' I shouted. But he didn't listen to me and didn't even look at me.

"Stop brother, I want to teach you Russian.

"I turned my flintlock around and whacked him on the nose with all my might. He roared and I stick my left arm in his teeth, my knife into his heart. He puts his claws on me—

"The blood rushes over me like a wave. A whole world sinks."

He sat for a while, holding his head in his hands, and remained silent.

Then he lightly hit the tabletop with the palm of his hand and said with a smile: "Well, I've gone and told you a real story. But you should see his claws. Let me open my shirt—" He undid it and showed me a scar on each side of his chest; it looked like the white impression on a giant's hand.

"He had a good hold on me."

The glasses were empty. I signaled to Moschku to bring us another glass.

"That's the way the peasants found me," my boyar continued. "But enough of that. So I lay with a fever for a long time in the Senkovs' house. When I would come to during the day, they'd be sitting around me, my people too, like at a death watch, but Father Senkov said: 'Things are getting better now!' and Nikolaya laughed. Once I woke up in the night and looked around me. There was just one lonely lamp burning. Nikolaya was on her knees praying.

"Enough of that. It's over. It just comes back in dreams sometimes. Enough. You can see that I didn't die.

"Now Father Senkov started coming over in his britschka[12] to see us and my father would return the visit. The women frequently came along. The old people would whisper, and if I joined them, Senkov would smile, his eyes would twinkle, and he'd offer me a pinch of tobacco.

"Nikolaya—loved me. With all her heart, believe me! I believed it at least, and the old people believed it too.

"And so she became my wife.

"My father turned the management of the estate over to me. Senkov gave his daughter a whole village.

"The wedding took place in Czernelica. Everybody was drunk, I'm telling you. My father danced the Cossack with Madame Senkov.

"The next evening—they were all still looking for their limbs like the dead on Judgment Day and not finding them—I hitched up six horses myself, all of them white as doves. The gleaming, long-haired pelt from my dead bear was spread out on the seat of my coach, the paws with gilded claws hanging down to the footboard on both sides, the big head with its sparkling eyes lying as if alive at our feet. My people— peasants, Cossacks on their horses with torches and burning branches in their hands—were all around us. I picked up my wife with her red ermine fur on her shoulder and lifted her into the coach. My people were jubilant. She was sitting like a queen in the bear's pelt, her little feet on his big head.

"And so, with my people on horseback around us, I brought the mistress to her home.—

"What you read in German books about love being like paradise is nonsense, and then there's the idolatry that they practice about virginity—"

"Like Schiller, for example, in—"

"Oh, please. You're really not going to recite something by Herr von Schiller. Have mercy—"

"Just one section, all right?"

"Forgive me—"

> "With the belt and with the veil
> fell the sweet deception."

I declaimed it without mercy.

"Well he's right for a change, old Herr von Schiller," my country nobleman said. "A sweet deception! That would really be something if a virgin were the crown of creation, and love were only the lovely, dumb feeling that you feel only for a girl like that. The sweet deception ended for me as well.

"When she had become my wife, I had the courage for the first time to love her, and the same was true for her. She threw decency and propriety on to the floor along with everything else, her corset and her garter belt, and my love grew ever greater in the presence of her love. My love and her love grew like twins.

"I kissed Pana Nikolaya's hands, my wife's feet, and I bit them so often that she screamed and kicked my face.

"I now understood why you would kneel down and worship a woman with child, but they made a virgin out of her, too, these domesticated pets of our dear Lord.

"You see, a girl is the slave of her house. Some fathers consider her to be part of their property. But a woman—she could leave me at any moment. Am I right? She chooses like I do. And they go and put a virgin on the altar for me to pray to. Really stupid. Then they say, 'You sweet child.' They want me to consider some butter-yellow duckling to be my equal. Do me a favor and think about that.

"The love between a man and a woman is what marriage is; I mean marriage the way that nature does it.

"After all, what else is there?

"Be so kind as to observe this life for a minute. A strange text and—"

He listened to the song of the peasant patrol for a few minutes.

"And then the melody that goes with it.

"The Germans have their Faust, and the English have a book like that.—Every one of our peasants knows what they do. They know what life is about as if by instinct.

"What makes our people so melancholy?

"The flatland.

"It pours itself out like the sea and waves in the wind like the sea. The stars set in it—like in the sea—it surrounds men as silently as infinity and is as alien as nature.

"We'd talk to it and get an answer from it if we could. That song tears itself from a man's breast like a cry of pain and dies unanswered as a sigh.

"Men feel so strange when that happens. Aren't they a part of nature? Didn't it create him? Did nature only triumph over them? Did they abandon nature? Does nature cast them from herself?

"Nature gives no answer.

"A tree grows from his grave, and sparrows screech from its branches. Is that supposed to be an answer?

"Men watch ants laden with eggs marching back and forth through the warm sand in long caravans. That's where they find their world. Creatures swarming in the smallest of spaces, an endless effort for the sake of—nothing. They feel abandoned, like they could forget at any moment that they are alive.

"Nature speaks to men through women: 'You are my child. You fear me like death, but I am here like you. Kiss me! I love you. Come and take part in creating the mystery of life that you fear. Come, I love you!'"

He was quiet for a while and then continued.

"Nikolaya and I, how happy we were! When our parents or neighbors came to visit, you should have seen how she ruled the house and how everyone obeyed her. The servants put their heads down like ducks in the water whenever she looked at them. Once my young Cossack threw a dozen plates onto the table—carried them in a pile right up to his chin and tossed them on the table. My wife grabbed the whip from the nail in the wall. Well—if the mistress will whip him, he says, he'll break a dozen plates every day. They both started to laugh.

"The neighbors came too.

"They always came to visit on the holy days, especially at Easter for the blessed meal,[13] but now they really came in droves. Everybody came, I'm telling you.

"There was Lieutenant Mack, retired, he knew Schiller by heart but was otherwise a good man. He suffered from the misfortune of liking to drink. I don't mean that he'd get so drunk that you could throw him under the sofa. You know, he stand up in the middle of the room, a small, fat, red-faced man, and recite for you the battle with the dragon, or when he was sober—picture this—he'd tell us about all the wars with the French. You tell me what you should do in a situation like that.

"Then there was the Baron Schebicki. Don't you know him? His old man was actually named Schebig, Salomon Schebig. He was a Jew who went around as a peddler buying and selling, served as a government supplier, bought an estate, and called himself Schebigstein. ' If someone can be called Lichtenstein,' he said, 'why shouldn't I be called Schebigstein?' And his son became a baron and calls himself Raphael Schebicki. He laughs all the time. If you say to him 'Do me the honor of visiting me'—he just laughs, and if you say 'There's the door,'!"[14]—he still laughs. And he always wants to bring every beautiful woman clothes from Brody[15] or a shawl from Paris. He never drinks anything but water, goes to the sauna every day, wears a large gold chain on his red velvet vest, and always makes the sign of the cross before soup and after dinner.

"Then there was the nobleman Domboski. A tall Pole with red eyes, a melancholy mustache and empty pockets. He's always collecting for the emigrants. Anyone he's seen twice, he'll press passionately to his chest and kiss tenderly. If he's had a glass too many, he'll spill uncounted tears, sing 'Poland is not yet lost,' take everyone by the arm, and betray the entire Polish conspiracy to them. When he finally cheers up, he'll toast you with 'Vivat, let us love one another,' and drink from the women's dirty shoes.

"Then there was the Reverend Mister Macziek, an honest country preacher who found comfort for everything, birth, death, and marriage. But he praised most highly those who take their eternal rest in the Lord. Even the church distinguishes them symbolically by charging a higher fee. Whenever he made a pronouncement he always said "purgatory" like others would say "by God" or "my word."

"There was also the learned Thaddeus Kuternoga, who'd been trying to finish his doctorate for eleven years, and picture this, it was in philosophy. Finally there was the estate owner Leon Bodoschkan, a true friend, and other merry aristocrats.

"Merry! As merry as a swarm of bees, but they respected her.

"The women came to visit her as well; good friends, they chatted, smiled sweetly, promised every minute, and then—well, we know how that is. So that's how we lived with the neighbors, and I was proud of my wife when they drank from her shoes and made their toasts to her. But she just looked at them all like this: 'Why are you making such an effort?'—We preferred being alone.

"It was such a big estate, you know. You have your cares and your joys. She really got involved in running it. We want to rule our realm ourselves, she said, and not hand it over to our ministers. One minister was our agent Kradulinski, an old Pole. He was a man of consequence, I'm telling you—he never had a hair on his head nor an invoice in order. Then there was Kreidel, the forester. A German, as you will have noticed. He was small, had little eyes, big, transparent ears, and a big transparent greyhound.

"My wife held them together like a team of horses. Well, I think she would have given them the whip if they hadn't driven the cart the way she wanted.

"And then there were the peasants, on the other hand. Whenever we walked through the fields, they'd say 'Praise be to Jesus Christ!' and 'Forever and ever, amen.' So happy, I'm telling you. During the harvest celebration, they would stream to our home, the reapers and the people. My wife would stand on the steps, and they'd lay the harvest wreath at her feet. They'd cheer, sing, dance, and she'd take a glass of brandy, shout 'May you stay healthy' and drink it in one gulp.

"I'm telling you, they would just kiss her feet.

"She'd also go riding with me. I'd hold my hand out for her, and she'd step on it and be right in the saddle. When she rode, she'd wear a Cossack cap with the golden tassel dancing on the back of her neck, and the horse would whinny and flare its nostrils when she patted it on the neck.

"Then I taught her to use a rifle. I had a really little one. I used it to shoot sparrows when I was little. She'd throw it over her shoulder and walk with me through the fields and shoot quail. It was magnificent, I'm telling you, magnificent!—Once a vulture came flying out of the forest and started taking my chickens, even took Nikolaya's black hen with the white tuft. I started to watch for him.

"One day I was coming back from digging potatoes, carrying a switch in my hand, and there he was.

"He's screeching and flying around the yard, and I can only curse. Suddenly there's a shot. He flaps his wings once and falls straight to the ground.

"Who fired the shot?

"My wife. 'He's not going to take any more of my hens,' she says and nails him to the barn door.

"Then the factor[16] would come and unpack all his bundles with a big commotion. 'Everything genuine, everything new, everything cheap.'—Did she know how to bargain!

"The Jew would just always sigh. 'A strict mistress,' he'd say, but then he'd kiss her elbow and drive off into town.

"The starost's[17] wife would come along wearing a blue dress with white bows. It must be the fashion, so I buy her a blue dress with white bows. My Nikolaya turned red.

"I went to Brody once and brought back velvet in all colors, silks, furs—what furs! All black. Her heart was beating, I can tell you.

"The way she dressed. It was enough to make you kneel down.

"She had a kazabaika,[18] a luscious green, a magnificent green, with Siberian gray squirrels on it—the Empress of Russia had no better—they were identical and as wide as a hand. All lined with silver-gray fur. Just so soft I'm telling you.

"She'd lie like that on the divan during the long evenings, her hands clasped behind her head, and I'd read to her.

"The fire would crackle, the samovar sing, the cricket chirp, the woodworm knock, and the mouse would chew away because the white cat was lying by the hearth dreaming.

"I read her all the novels. In the district capital, you know, there was already a lending library, and then the neighbors—this one would have a book or that one.

"She'd lie there with her eyes closed, and I'd be in the lounge chair, and we'd just consume the books. We often wouldn't be able to fall asleep for a long time. We'd talk about whether this guy would get this girl or not. Whenever some act of magnanimity was called for in the story, Nikolaya's earlobes would turn red with anger. She'd sit up, lean on her hand, and say, as if I had written it: 'Don't let her do that, hear?'—and almost cry.

"Women, you know, are especially magnanimous in novels. When their lover is in danger, they're right there, ready to—sacrifice themselves. Can you imagine? Once a scene like that took place where a woman gave up her husband to save her child. A dumb story, I'm telling you. 'The Power of a Mother's Love,' I think, was the title of the book. A dumb story, but Nikolaya got feverish and didn't want to see a book for weeks after that.

"She'd often jump up, hit me in the face with the book, and stick out her tongue. We'd chase each other around like children. I'd hide behind doors and scare her.

"Or she'd act out whole fairy tales with me.

"She'd go to her room. 'When I come back, you'll be my slave.' And she'd dress up as a female sultan, wrap a scarf around her hips and another around her head like a turban. She'd come out with my Circassian dagger in her sash, wrapped completely in a white veil. What a woman! A Goddess of a woman!"

"When she slept, I could spend hours looking at her, watching her breathe, and if she would sigh, I'd feel such a strong pain in my heart, just as if I had done her the worst injustice, and I'd be overcome with the fear that she wasn't mine, that she had died. And I'd call her by name, and she'd sit up, look at me with her eyes wide open and laugh.

"But it was the sultan game that she played best. Not a muscle in her face would twitch. If I'd say: 'But Nikolaya,' and joke, she'd just lift her eyebrows and drill her eyes into me so that I almost felt as if I were already at the stake. 'Are you mad, slave?'—Really, there was nothing that I could do. I was her slave, and she ruled me like a sultan.

"And so we lived like a couple of swallows perched together and chirping.

"Our joys were heightened by a sweet expectation. And yet, how afraid I was for my wife. I'd often just push her hair out of her forehead and get tears in my eyes. She'd understand me and put her arms around my neck and cry.

"But it came as unexpectedly as good fortune. I rode into Kolomea for the doctor, and when I returned, she was holding the child out toward me.

"Our parents literally melted with joy, and the servants shouted and laughed, and everyone was drunk, and a stork stood on top of the barn with one leg held thoughtfully in the air.

"That gave us things to think about, to worry about, and every difficult hour just bound us more closely to one another.

"But it didn't stay that way."

His voice had become infinitely gentle and quiet. It just quivered in the air, as quiet as the thin smoke of his pipe.

"It couldn't stay like that—you see—and then—this and that—you see what I'm saying? It's a kind of rule.—I mean, it's nature. I've often thought about it. What do you think?

"I had a friend—Leon Bodoschkan. He read too much, and it made him ill. He often said to me—"

"But why am I telling you that? I can show you—"

He pulled a few yellowed strips of paper from inside his coat.

"He wrote a lot, too. He was so unknown, but he knew everything. He'd see right down to the bottom of things as if they were a mountain stream. He opened people up and looked in to see if everything was in order as if they were watches. He'd tell you right away what was wrong. He'd understand what the cats were saying to each other, and he'd laugh and tell you right off what they wanted. He'd take a flower, cut it open, and show you how it lived, how it nourished itself. He liked to talk about women.

"Women and philosophy, you know. That's what ruined him.

"He'd often write something down, and when he'd go for a walk in the woods, he'd throw it all away. Paper scared him.

"But I'd forget otherwise.

"He said that if you wrote your love down on paper, you weren't in love.

"He could read thick books bound in leather, all of Nestor's works—but he'd run away from a love letter.

"So, for example—"

With that, he laid his dirty paper strips on the table.

"No! That's a bill." He stuck it back in his pocket. "There it is." He coughed and then read:

"'What is our life? Suffering, doubt, fear, despair.

"'Do you know where you come from? Who you are? Where you're going?

"'And to have no power over nature, to receive no answer to these poor, desperate questions. Suicide, ultimately, is the sum of our wisdom.

"'But nature has given us a sorrow that's more horrifying than life—love.

"'People call it a joy, call it lust—'

"My friend was always in the habit of laughing bitterly when he got to this passage.—'Look at the wolf,' he said to me, 'when he's looking for his mate, how he breaks through the undergrowth, the water dripping from his mouth. He doesn't even howl any longer, he just whimpers; and his love, is that a pleasure? It's a struggle, a struggle as if for life itself. The blood just runs from its neck.

"'My God! Wouldn't men just like to throw themselves upon women like they do upon their enemies? Doesn't he feel endlessly subjugated to a merciless enemy?

"'Doesn't he lay his proud head down at a woman's feet and plead: Kick me, kick me with your foot; I want to be your slave, your lackey, but come and save me!

"'Yes, love is sorrow and pleasure is salvation! But then it is a power that one exercises over the other. It's a competition to subjugate oneself to the other. Love is slavery, and you become a slave when you love. You feel abused by a woman and only revel in the ecstasy of her despotism and cruelty. You kiss the foot that kicks you.

"'A woman that I love scares me. I tremble when she suddenly walks through the room and her clothing rustles. A movement that surprises me scares me.

"'You'd like to marry for eternity, for this world and the other. You'd like to flow into each other. You submerge your soul in the soul of another, you descend into the depths of a strange, inimical nature and receive your baptism. It's absurd, quite absurd that the two of you haven't always been together. You tremble every second with the fear of losing each other. You are scared when the other's eyes close or voice changes. You'd like to be just one creature. You'd like to tear all the characteristics, ideas, and sacred beliefs out of your very being in order to merge completely with the other. You surrender yourself—like a thing—like a substance. Make of me what you are!

"'As if committing suicide, you throw yourself into the other's nature until your own rebels.

"'You feel the shudder of losing yourself completely. You feel something like hatred toward the power of the other. You think yourself dead. You want to rise up against the tyranny of the other's life and find your way back to your self.

"'That is the resurrection of nature.'"

He pulled out a second piece of paper.

"'The man has his work, his plans, his actions, his ideas!

"'They surround him like doves and raise him up like eagles. They keep him from sinking.

"'But the woman?

"'She cries for help. Her ego doesn't want to die, it doesn't! And there is no help!

"'But then she carries his image under her heart, feels it growing and moving—living! And then—she finally holds it in her arms. She lifts it up—

"'What does she feel now?

"'Is she dreaming? Then the child speaks to her: I am you, and you live in me; look at me, for I shall save you.

"'She holds the child to her breast and is saved.

"'Now she cares for her self in her child, the self that she had despised and rejected, and sees it grow on her lap, and she surrenders herself to it completely and is dependent on it.'"

With that he gathered up his friend's thoughts and hid them away. He felt for them with the palm of his hand once more and buttoned up his coat.

"That's the way it was for me, too," he said. "Just like that. Of course, I can't explain it as well as Leon Bodoschkan, you know, but I want to tell you about it. What do you think?"

"Of course, brother."

"It was just like that for me, too. Just like that. Believe me, just like that—"

I wanted to provoke my new friend and said cold-bloodedly: "Usually a child is seen as a pledge of love."

My rural nobleman was silent for a moment and looked as if I had mortally insulted him. "A pledge of love!" he cried. "Yes, indeed, a pledge of love.

"So I come home at night. There's a lot of work on an estate like that. I come home as tired as a hunting dog. I take my wife in my arms, kiss her, her hand strokes the worries away from my forehead. I rub up against her like a cat, she laughs—and the pledge of love next to her starts screaming—that's the end of that story. You can start again at the foreword if you want. That's the end of that, I'm telling you.

"You rush around like a madman all morning with the agent, the foreman, the forester. You sit down to dinner and barely get your napkin tied around your neck—I tie it, you see, everything in the old style—when the pledge of love starts to cry because it doesn't want the serving girl to feed it. My little wife gets up and feeds the child. But the child wants the real thing and screams—so off into the next room, and I can eat alone and whistle a little song to myself if I want, like this one:

> Sits the cat
> Up on the bough.
> All he does
> Is cry meow!
> Hey, my song
> Sure ain't long.[19]

"All you can do is—go duck hunting.

"Standing in water up to your knees all day long. You look forward to a good bed.

"What do you consider to be a good bed?

"A good mattress, right? Good padding, warm blankets, a pretty wife?"

He blushed and murmured something.

"All well and good. You kiss your little wife until she has red spots on her cheeks, neck, breasts. You let your hands run down her full hips—and the pledge of love screams.

"The wife jumps out of the bed, slips into her shoes, and walks back and forth, rocking the child in her arms. La! La! La! You hear it for half the night, and you sleep—alone. La! La! La!

"A year goes by.

"Everybody feels strange. There's something in the air. Everybody feels it, and nobody can name it.

"You see strange faces. The Polish estate owners ride back and forth. One man buys a horse, another gunpowder. At night you see a fiery band of light in the skies. The peasants stand in groups in front of the tavern and say that that means war or cholera or revolution.

"Worry overtakes you. All at once you feel that you have a fatherland that has sunk its border posts deep into the Slavic, the German, and other peoples' earth. 'What do the Polacks want?' you think and worry about the Austrian eagle in front of the district office and worry about your barn. You walk around your house at night to see if anyone has set any fires to it.

"You need to talk.

"Who with? Your wife. Ha, ha, ha! The pledge of love really howls because there's a fly sitting on his nose.

"I walk out in front of the house.

"The horizon is fiery red. A peasant rides past and shouts: 'Revolution!' and spurs his skinny horse on.

"They begin ringing the alarm in the village.

"A peasant starts nailing his scythe, and two more come with their flails across their shoulders.

"Others enter the yard.

"'Sir! We have to take precautions—the Poles are coming.' I load my pistols and have my saber sharpened.

"'My wife, give me a ribbon for my cap, a rag for all I care—as long as it's black and yellow!'—Ha, ha, ha! What do you think?—'Get out,' she says. 'My baby's crying, it's dying. Ride into the village and make them stop ringing those bells! Get out!'—Oho! Now things are different, and I have them ring the alarm in all the villages. Let the brat scream, you know? The country's in danger.

"But I'm telling you. All well and good.

"Finally we're together. We're just sitting on the divan. I've got my arm around her. She's listening to see if the child is moving. 'What did you say?' she asks after a while. 'Nothing,' I say. 'Nothing.' But my heart is heavy, I assure you.

"'Where's your kazabaika, Nikolaya?'—'Oh, it's in the house with the child.'—Yes, of course. Her hair is combed in any old way, and she puts on the first dress she sees in the morning. Who's going to get dressed up to stay in the house? Of course!—I often don't recognize her pretty face anymore. But the child—you know? 'When I get dressed up, the child doesn't recognize me. Can't you understand that?'—'Of course, I understand everything, everything.' But when guests are there, you know, the child can cry all it wants. She'll run in to it for a minute, then she'll pour the tea and laugh and chat, because our people would do anything for guests.

"Oho! That's when you get to see the green jacket lined with Siberian squirrel again. 'I have to dress up for our company.' You see! —I go bear hunting for the first time in a long time. My wife is rocking the child, and when I kiss her, she says: 'Go away, you'll wake the baby.' What do I do? I go away.

"My gamekeeper has seen the bear—but I almost went off and told you an anecdote again. All right. We were in danger, the gamekeeper and I. A peasant ran on ahead of us to the house.

"There was a tumult in the house when we got there, I can tell you. My wife throws her arms around my neck. She brings me the baby.

"The blood, you know, is running from the top of my head—the baby screams.—'Go away.'"

He shrugged his shoulders with contempt.

"The little bit of blood wasn't worth talking about, neither were the poor little child's tears but—for me the danger had passed—women are very practical. Okay, I wash the blood off me. The gamekeeper, an old soldier, bandages me. But what do you think? The pledge of love begins screaming when it sees the white bandage. 'Get out, out! The baby's going to get hiccups! Out!'—So what are you going to do? You throw yourself on your bed and stay there a while, alone, like before you'd gotten to know a woman.

"The devil take the pledge of love! God forgive me my sin." He made the sign of the cross and spat with defiance.

"I spread the bearskin out in front of the bed for my wife. What do you think? She starts to shout, 'Get that skin out of here, it reminds me of when the baby was afraid.' Just think—it doesn't remind her of my blood or the danger I was in. Oh, women are practical, damned practical."

"Forgive me," I said, "did you ever tell your wife—"

"Oh, please," he interrupted me almost vehemently. His nostrils were quivering.

"I told her. What do you think her answer was? 'Well, good. Then why have children?' Do you think she would have been capable—we are the slaves of our wives. You don't want to run right out and cheat on her. Or become a monk. What's left except to let yourself be abused. Oh, there was a time when I was ready to take the child and—you know what I mean?

"For example, a scene like this one.

"It's early and I'm smoking my pipe, a long Turkish one like the one there, with an open wire cover. The baby immediately wants the fire and starts crying. I let it cry. My wife is already burning up. 'Let him have it already.' She means the amber piece. But I hold out the glowing red pipe to him. He grabs it and screams and cries.

"'Jesus Mary, the poor child!' I just told my wife to have a good time, and I went out to the fields with my gun and could have laughed myself to death about the fact that she's back there with a crying child with burnt fingers.

"In those days I no longer thought like that. What am I talking about! You do what you can. But—think about it yourself. For example, did you ever have a clock suddenly stop on you? A wall clock? Well, of course you have. Do you get impatient?"

"Sometimes."

"Good, so you're impatient. You want the clock to work. Right now. So you give it a shove, at least the pendulum. All right, it works. But for how long? It stops again. — And again. — And again. Well, you get impatient. You really give it a shove. Good, now it's stopped for good.

"That's just the way it goes when you try to get your heart to work right.

"You love your wife, and you want more than just your bed.

"You see, it's like a pain when you long for your wife. But then it passes.

"You see, you've been released, nothing else.

"You see that that's really nothing, that there's something more than that, that a man and woman are different from male and female wolves. But it was all for nothing.

"Assume my wife was a book. I'd like to read this book all the way to the end. But I keep having to start over. Finally I slam it shut. Let somebody else read it all the way through.—

"In the beginning, brother, I just wanted to be entertained, you understand?

"The cavalry was all over the place.

"I decided to make the acquaintance of the officers. What people they were! Banay, for example, you know him?"

"No."

"Or Baron Pál? Him either? But Nemethy with the pointy mustache—surely you knew him!

"So we'd go visit one or the other of them.

"But they were at my house almost daily. We'd smoke and drink our Russian tea. Somebody would tell a story. Finally we'd play some cards.

"We'd go out hunting together a lot, too. I learned how to shoot snipe in those days.

"Well, my wife noticed all this. She came to me and sat down and was quiet and finally started reproaching me. I just said: 'My love, what do I have at home? By the way, your baby's screaming.' The next time, my Nikolaya shows up in her green kazabaika with the silver gray squirrel fur, her hair really done up, and sits right down in the middle of the officers.

"I laugh. She wants to make me jealous. She turns this way and that, jokes, and purrs. She doesn't even look at me. My cavalry officers, you know, had honorable bones in their bodies; there was no question about that. And second, none of them felt like dying—and why should they?—or putting themselves in danger, or becoming a cripple. For what? The only way you'll do that is if you love a woman so much that none of that matters.

"But they tease me. 'What do you think, brother, of your wife courting us like that?' 'Just court her right back.' But around that time another man started coming to the house. You don't know him.

"I couldn't stand him right from the start. So blond, you know, and very white, an estate owner. Had his butler curl his hair for him every day, read Igor[20] aloud and Pushkin, and immediately acted out what he declaimed—a real actor, I'm telling you.

"Anyway, I didn't like him. But my wife did."

His voice had become hoarse. The more agitated he became, the more he suppressed his voice. It came out of his chest constricted and deep.

"But that comes later.

"It was a fun life in those days.

"In the winter, the estate owners would also come over with their wives. There would be dances, masquerades, sleigh rides, everything, just everything!

"Even my wife would have a good time.

"Then she had a second child in the summer. Another boy, two boys.

"So harmony was somewhat restored.

"Once I said to Nikolaya—I was sitting on her bed and tucking her in when she rolled over—'Please, take pity on me. Hire a nanny for the baby.' She shook her head. What do I do? Tears come to my eyes, and I leave the room. It was all in vain.

"Nikolaya occupied herself with the baby again almost for a whole year. We rarely spoke with each other.

"The result was that when I wanted to tell her something, I had to make long introductions to the topic, and my wife began to be bored with me. She'd yawn over and over again, and her eyes would cloud over. Then it became obvious how easily we'd begin to fight. She always wanted to be right.

"If I preferred one of the servants, he'd be chased right out of his job. With a scene, of course. Or I'd find that the blue kerchief looked especially good on her. Right. Next Sunday the housekeeper would be wearing it in church.

"And always in front of strangers. That's really so unpleasant. You don't want to always be arguing with your wife and besides—you're a man. And when she always takes other people's sides. I'm always wrong and the other one is always right. What do you think about that?"

He spat mightily to one side.

"Or even—I explain to her, 'Dear Nikolaya, don't do that to me. Have pity.' Right, she keeps quiet the next time. —'And you, madam, what do you think?' —'Me? I say what my husband says.' As nasty as a Tartar!

"She has to force herself to agree with me, you see! When I think about it, I don't understand how I'm still alive.

"Suddenly I lost a large sum of money. We kept things up, you know, and I, of course, had some bad luck—while gambling. Once I lost all my cash, horses, and carriage."

He laughed heartily about it.

"Good. I take myself by the hand and say: you made a bad job of it. Pulled myself back in an honorable fashion. Friends and neighbors stayed away.

"Then he came.

"It doesn't worry me anymore, you know. Back then I began running the estate myself, was lucky sometimes, and when you see things you've planted growing at your feet, so to speak, that gets you interested in a way. And besides, farming is like gambling. You make your plan like when you gamble, you have to know how to change it at any given moment based on the circumstances, and chance also plays a role: storms, hail, frost, drought, disease, locusts.

"When I come in for tea and fill my pipe, I remember that the horse needs to be shod or I should check the orchard to see what's stronger, my watchman there or my brandy. I take my cap and go off again, and I don't even realize that my wife is sitting with the children.

"People started talking about it already. 'It's like any other marriage.' Even the Reverend Macziek brought great consolation to me. His face, his hair were glistening with oil—it must have been holy—as was the collar on his jacket. The oil even extended to his boots and his elbows. He was shining like a cherub. He raised his yellow cane over my head like a shepherd's staff, and he raised his voice even higher. 'But, Reverend, what if we don't love each other anymore, my wife and I?' — 'Oho! Purgatory! That's just it,' and he laughed so much that his reverend stomach and the oiled cheeks shook. 'Oho, purgatory! That's just what a Christian marriage is.' — 'But, Reverend, should we live like that? That's just not possible.' — 'Oho, purgatory! Of course that's not possible. What would we need the church for otherwise? You know what Christianity is, my dear, confused friend?

"'When you have your way with a young woman without loving her, what will people say? The degenerate! In a Christian marriage, it's not a problem.

"'Or if you pay a young lady or give her something like a scarf, whatever, it leaves a bad taste in everyone's mouth. That girl there is selling herself! In the Christian marriage, my confused friend, that's not a problem.

"'For what does a good Christian wife speak of? Pleasures like the ones I've just mentioned? Purgatory! She speaks of her dowry, and how her good, Christian spouse clothes and feeds her. Am I right?

"'Love? Marriage says: Care for your wife, feed your children, and in return—you get your bed. Basta! That's a Christian marriage. Purgatory, that's what I think.

"'So it's a great scandal when a girl falls in love and has a child. Ridiculous! But if you're married—even if you spit on yourself once a day—it's considered a blessing from God!

"'Do you marry for love or for the blessing of a priest? Well? If you wanted to marry for love, you wouldn't need the priest's blessing. Ergo! That's what I think!' That was the pastor's way of thinking.

"I start feeling more and more lonely at home, and I can't resist the urge to go out.

"I stay outside in the fields when the reaping is being done and sit down when the sheaves are standing, as if in a tent. I smoke and listen to the people singing. I go off into the forests when they cut wood and shoot a squirrel. There isn't a market in the whole district that I wouldn't go to. I even ride to Lemberg often, especially during contract time.[21] I stay away from home for weeks.

"You can understand that with my wife I only—you know—in short, that we lead a Christian marriage.

"My neighbor, however, doesn't understand that at all. He thinks he can have his heart prettied up every day like his hair. He spends half the day sitting with my wife, especially when I'm not home. When I go to the fair or off on the hunt—he's right there.

"'Isn't my friend'—he was in the habit of calling me that, so let's let it go—'Isn't my friend at home?' — 'No.' — 'I'm very sorry about that.'

"Remember that—the polecat—and he sits down and recites Pushkin.

"Then in the conversation: 'But he's never at home. Hm.' — 'Never.' — He just shakes his head and my wife—oh, God, you know how it is—she picks up the complaint and goes with it. They make allusions, and he just keeps shaking his head and inhaling sympathetically through his nose. Talks about men in general, so instructively and so entertainingly, you know. And he doesn't even trust himself to spit firmly—he just coughs a little something into his handkerchief.

"He makes a scene with me about my neglecting my wife. And what a wife! A beautiful woman, a woman who has such a soul, she's pure soul, and an intelligent, witty woman who reads Pushkin as if it were a prayerbook.

"That's easy to say. You have her at the samovar, my friend, in her squirrel fur, and as lively as a squirrel, too. But me! — Ah! Let's let that go.

"She has him read whole books aloud to her, gets ideas from them, and sighs when they talk about me.

"And what is the problem, actually? What have we done to each other? — 'We don't understand each other,' she says.

"You know, word for word from a German book. Word for word, I'm telling you. So much for those ideas.

"One night I came home from an auction in Dobromil, you know.

"My wife is sitting on the divan, her one foot up, holding her knee with her hands, just lost in herself.

"My friend had just been there—my wife is wearing her squirrel fur jacket and then—I smell him. For a moment, I'd like to let myself get angry, but I let it go. My wife looks so pleasing to me that I kiss her hands and stroke the fur on her jacket. Suddenly she looks at me, a look that was so strange that I was astonished by it.

"'Things can't go on like this,' she says. Quite suddenly. Her voice was quite hoarse. Then she forced herself to speak loudly. — 'What's the matter?' — 'You only come to me at night,' she begins shouting. 'People at least court their mistresses, and I—I want love!'

"'Love? Don't I love you?' — 'No!'

"She saddles her horse and gallops off.

"I look for her the whole night, the whole day.

"When I come home, her bed is in the children's room, and I sleep alone.

"I should have made a scene myself, that's true—but—I was too proud. I thought it would take care of itself.

"Then there were the women from the vicinity. There was a German clerk at the district office. His wife is getting love letters from a cavalry officer. 'What do you have there, my love?' He takes the letter out of her hand, reads it, and right away he beats his wife. Beats her until she leaves the house—what am I saying?—he beats her until she loves him again. That was a happy marriage.

"But me—I was just a slave. If only I had created a scene back then. But none of that matters now.

"We'd say 'good morning' and 'good night' to each other, and that was all. Good night! Those were some nights. I could have had myself declared a saint every day!

"Then I started going hunting again.

"I was in the forests for whole days at a time.

"There was a gamekeeper back then. His name was Irena Wolk. A strange man. He loved all living things. He'd just quiver when he'd discover an animal, and yet he'd kill every one of them.

"Then he'd hold it in his hand, look at it, and say with such a sad voice: 'He's fine now, he's fine!'

"He considered life to be a misfortune. I don't know. A strange man. But I'll tell you about him some other time.

"So I'd put a piece of bread and cheese in my torba,[22] fill my hunting flask, and head out.

"We'd usually lie down at the edge of the forest.

"Irena would go off into the field, dig a few potatoes out, make a fire, and bake them in the ashes. You eat what you have.

"When you wander like that through the quiet, dark, high mountain forest, and you encounter wolves and bears; you see the eagle with its young; you breathe the damp, heavy, cool forest air with its bitter aroma; you use a felled tree for your dinner table; you sleep in a mountain cave and bathe in a dark lake that has no bottom and no waves and a smooth, pitch-dark surface that swallows the sun's rays like the light of the moon—then you no longer have any feelings. The feelings turn into desires. You eat because of hunger and you make love from instinct.

"The sun goes down. Irena's hunting for mushrooms.

"A peasant woman is sitting on the ground.

"Her dull blue skirt doesn't hide her small, dusty feet. Her dirty blouse is falling halfway off her shoulders, and the way it's belted over her skirt leaves her breasts visible.

"There is the aroma of thyme around her. With her elbows resting on her knees, she's holding her head in both her hands and just staring off into the distance. A firefly settled in her hair, which, uncombed, just flowed down her back from under her red kerchief.

"From the side, her face stood out almost darkly against the red evening sky, so sharply as to look like a cut-out. Her nose is curved and fine, like that of a bird of prey, and when I call out to her, she even utters a cry like that of a mountain vulture, and her eyes hiss out at me. For a moment, her gaze floats over her eyes like a naphtha flame.

"Her cry continues to resonate—the steep cliff echoes it, the thick forest returns it once more, and the distant mountains send it back yet again.

"I'm almost frightened by the woman.

"She bends down, picks some thyme, and yanks the red kerchief down over her glowing red face.

"'What's the matter?' I ask.

"She doesn't answer, but pours out the melancholy sounds of a duma[23] into the air like tears.

"'What's the matter with you?' I say. 'Are you in pain, in mourning?' — She remains silent. — 'Well, what's bothering you?'

"She looks me in the eye, laughs, and lets her long eyelashes fall back over her eyes like dark veils.

"'What can I do for you?' — 'Bring me a sheepskin,' she says softly. I laugh. 'Wait, I will bring you one from the market.' — She hides her face. — 'But you'll stink in it, a new sheepskin like that. You know what? I'll bring you a sukmana. What do you think? With rabbit fur, black—or white, milky white—"

"She looked at me with amazement, not a bit seriously, narrowed her eyes a bit, and her lips just danced around her big, white teeth. Then, slowly, beginning with the corners of her mouth and her cheeks, a scampish laugh suddenly flashed across her whole face.

"'Well, what are you laughing about? — No answer. — 'Well tell me, do you want the sukmana? No? How about the rabbit fur, the milk-white rabbit fur?'

"Suddenly she stands up, straightens her skirt, pulls her blouse down.

"'No!' she says. 'If you want to give me something, it should have silver fur.' — 'Why silver?' — 'Like the fine ladies wear.'

"I just looked at her.

"Selfishness lay upon her face as sunny as innocence. It kissed her soul, her desires, as unconsciously as she would kiss an icon. There were no principles or even ideas involved. She had the morality of a hawk and the laws of the forest. She had no more Christianity than a young cat that occasionally wipes its nose with its paw.

"I really did bring her the sukmana from Lemberg and—you'll think I'm ridiculous—

"I fell in love with the woman.

"It was quite a romance—you'll never find its equal.

"As soon as I'd fire a shot—she'd be there.

"I'd comb her hair with my fingers and wash her feet in the mountain stream, but she'd splash me in the face with the water.

"She was a strange creature.

"There was something cruel about her coquettishness. She tormented me with the deepest humility in a way that a fine lady's arrogance never could.

"'Oh, have mercy, sir! My gracious master! Whatever shall I do with you?' — And in the end, she could do with me whatever she wanted."

We both said nothing for some time.

The peasants and the church singer had left the tavern. The Jew had put on his prayer straps and had then fallen asleep. Dreaming, he sang softly through his nose and nodded his head in time to the music.

His wife was sitting by the bar. Her head had sunk into her hands, she had stuck her little fingers between her teeth, and her sleepy eyes were half closed, but her gaze still hung on the stranger.

He put his pipe away and took a deep breath.

"Shall I tell you about the scene with my wife? You can spare me that.

"Afterwards, my wife was sickly for some time.

"I stayed at home and read. Once she walked through the room and softly said 'good night.' I stood up, but she was already gone—you could hear her door clicking into the lock. It was past.—

"At that time I was involved in a case with the Osnovian estate.

"Before you hitch up the court and let the lawyer drive, I thought, hitch up your horses and go over there yourself.

"What do I find? A divorced woman living on her estate because she found the great world repulsive, a modern female philosopher.

"She called herself Satana and was the most charming little devil. She'd just jump right up whenever a word was spoken, and she had eyes like will-o'-the-wisps.

"I lost the case, of course, but in return I won her heart, her kisses, and her bed.

"I still loved my wife.

"I often lay in another woman's arms and closed my eyes and made myself believe that it was her long, damp hair and her hot-blooded, feverish lips.

"In the meantime, my wife was feverish with love and hate towards me. Her heart was like one of those flowers that bloom in the shade, and now it simply spilled over with wild tenderness. She was inventive in betraying herself by trying too hard to conceal herself. One day she laid on the table in front of me a letter that my lover's Cossack had brought, and she laughed out loud—but her laughter broke off right in the middle in such a way that it was almost ugly.

"Because of an excess of love I turned away from her, and she yearned for revenge because of her passionate, rejected love.

"Wherever she went, it was in haste. She cried out in her dreams, and she slapped the servants and the children.

"Suddenly she changed.

"She seemed composed, contented. Her eye rested on me with such strange fulfillment, and yet pain flashed through her proud laughter.

"My gamekeeper came.

"'The master no longer visits the forest. I know where there's a fox over by the mossy run and where there are some big snipe,'—I was especially fond of shooting them, you see—'and she—she waits for you at the rock. Do the poor woman a kindness.'

"I took my rifle and went with him as far as the last fence in the village.

"There a nameless fear gripped me, and I left my gamekeeper and almost ran home.

"I was almost ashamed—I was walking softly on my tiptoes—when I heard—"

He brushed the hair from his forehead several times.

"It's not something you can tell. I tore the door open, and my wife was lying— 'Am I disturbing you?' I asked and closed the door again

"What did I do?

"I did what our people do. The German, of course, treats his wife like an underling, but we negotiate with her on an equal footing, like one monarch with another.

"We don't think: 'You can do what you want. The woman has no choice but to be satisfied.' Among our people, the husband has no privileges. We have only one set of rights for husband and wife.

"If you chuck every tavern maid under the chin, you have to put up with everyone paying your wife pleasantries. If you lie in the arms of a strange woman, then be silent when your wife embraces another.

"So did I have any rights?

"No, I didn't.

"So I left the room and walked back and forth in front of my wife's door.

"In reality, I felt nothing at all. Everything was as if frozen and quiet, very quiet.

"I said to myself over and over: 'Didn't you do the same thing? You have no rights, you have no rights.'

"Then he came out.

"I said: 'I didn't want to disturb you, my friend, but did you know that this is my house?' — He trembled, and so did his voice.

"'Do with me whatever you want,' he said.

"'What should I do with you? — Do you have any conception of honor? — We'll have to exchange a few shots.'

"I lit the way down the steps for him, and then I rode over to Leon Bodoschkan's. I wanted him to be my second.

"He gave me a gloomy smile. 'It's really a piece of stupidity,' he said, 'but everything will be taken care of by tomorrow morning. Just do me the favor of reading this manuscript tonight.' And with that he gave me these papers, you see, and I've carried them with me ever since. He's a strange man.

"So I read them.

"For what?

"I challenged my wife's lover to a duel, but that actually had no significance.

"I was in the wrong, I knew it. But honor—well, you know. But none of it meant anything.

"I knew that he wouldn't hit me. He couldn't tell a barn from a sparrow at fifteen paces—and I—well, I'm a good shot.

"I could take revenge. I could kill him. — Nobody would have said a word—but I had no right to do it and shot off to one side. Because I was, as I've already said, just as guilty as he or my wife.

"Back then I thought about separating from my wife. But the children! That's just it. They shackle us together in pairs for eternity and drive us forth into the whirlwind like the damned in Dante's hell.

"Have you ever considered how nature tricks us with love? Perhaps you'll let me—oh, what did I want to say? — Right —in essence, men and women are created only to be enemies. I hope you won't misunderstand me.

"Nature wants to propagate our race. What else would it want. We, however, are vain and gullible enough to convince ourselves that it has our happiness in mind.

"Yes—they're as incompatible as fish and poppies—as soon as there is a child, that's the end of happiness and love, too, and man and wife look at each other like two people who've made a bad trade. Both of them are deceived, and yet neither has betrayed the other. But they continue to believe that their happiness is the only important thing, and they feud with each other instead of accusing nature, which has given us, besides love, which is so transitory, another feeling that never ends: love for one's children.

"So we stayed together.

"He never entered my house again, but they would meet at an acquaintance's house. There are such good souls in the world. And I went back to shooting snipe.

"After that I began looking at women as some kind of game whose hunting was more difficult, but also more rewarding.

"Do you know how to shoot snipe? No? You have to know how snipe fly.

"They fly up, beat their wings three times, like a will-o'-the-wisp, zig! zag! and then straight ahead.

"That's the moment. I aim straight ahead, and the snipe is mine.

"Women are somewhat like that.

"If you fire right away—it's over. But if you have the right speed, you'll get every one.

"There was peace at home.

"The children were running around, and just imagine—I came to like them. I loved them because my wife loved them.

"I often thought that they were our love come to life, running around, playing, and laughing. And I began to feel strange.

"It came over me like some kind of evil. I demanded that the children should like me better than their mother, that they should love only me.

"I'd take them over to the fireplace, let them ride on my knee, tell them fairy tales, sing songs that they sing in the villages, tell them stories like the ones, for instance, that a hunter tells. And that was really strange. I had, you see—that is to say—you know what I'm trying to say? I'd gotten another child, it was another man's child. A girl. You wouldn't believe how much she looked like my wife, exactly like her.

"People usually say that girls look like their father, the sons like the mother. That wasn't my experience. The one boy is like his grandfather. I don't know where to put the other—my wife got him from a novel. Neither of my sons has anything from their mother, but the—other child, the girl.

"Was it because back then she thought of nothing but herself and her revenge?

"Well, the child was attached to me with its love and yet knew that I hated it.

"When I would tell stories, she would quietly ask permission and sit on a small stool in the dark corner and listen, and only her eyes would glow.

"I often screamed at her so much that she would start shaking. When I'd go away, she would stand in the distance and watch me go. When I'd come back, she'd run toward me, and then be surprised by her own actions.

"Once one of the boys said: 'The bear's going to kill father yet.' — She jumped up and her eyes were full of tears.

"It was as if it were my wife, pressing herself anxiously on me, begging me for forgiveness and crying for me.

"Once I said to the child: 'Come over here to me.' She turned red and purple and ran away. Slowly we became the best of friends.

"Neither of my boys was like me.

"'Would you like to go shooting fox?' — 'Yes,' said the boy, 'I would, if the gun didn't make so much noise.'

"Or when I'd tell them about a bear I'd seen: 'He was coming right at me. What do you think I did?' The boy said: 'You ran away.' But the girl only laughed.

"She'd often take a wolf's pelt and scare the two of them, and they'd run off and hide under their mother's skirt.

"'Don't you recognize your sister?' — 'Mother,' they'd say, 'she really is a wolf, her eyes flash and the way she howls is a pleasure to hear.'

"When I was away, the girl would wander restlessly about the whole house. 'I hope father doesn't get thrown.' — 'Why should he get thrown? — 'Oh, I know the Wallachian horses, the brown ones; they're wild animals. Or if the bear —' — 'Father will shoot him right in the white patch on his chest,' my boy said expertly. 'What if he misses?' — 'He won't miss.'

"When the girl got older, she'd throw herself on the ground and roll around and cry.

"So I finally took her along with me.

"I had that small rifle. My wife had used it for shooting. I bought her a hunting bag and took her along.

"The girl had courage, I can tell you, courage like a man. No, not like a man. How can I explain that to you?

"When we'd hear something coming through the brush, I'd say: 'Well, what if things go badly for us?' She'd just laugh. 'I'm here with you.' She was only scared for me.

"At home she would be feverish with anxiety, but faced with the wolf she was as calm as with a hen, I'm telling you. And how well we understood each other.

"I barely needed to speak, so well did she know my eye, my face, and my every gesture.

"And yet we so enjoyed speaking with each other.

"When the animal was lying there, Irena kneeling by it and gutting it, we'd sit together, and the world was like a picture book that I was showing my child—and she wasn't my child at all! But it was her child and I loved her.

"My wife also loved the child passionately, and the more devoted the child became to me, the more passionately she loved her.

"When I would take the child along with me, she would kneel down, kiss her, and say softly: 'Stay here with me.' But she would shake her head. I would laugh, and far away from the house in the depths of the forest, I would still remember the scene and be glad that the child was with me and the mother was at home, dying with fear.

"When my wife would give the girl something to sew, she'd only pretend to do it and would suddenly put it down and run off—to clean my rifle. Or my wife would say something to her. The child would look at me and not budge.

"Once my wife began shouting: 'He's not your father!'

"'Then you're not my mother,' the girl said calmly. My wife turned pale, was silent after that, and would only cry now and again. 'What nonsense! Who would want to waste their tears? The world is so much fun!'"

He tossed back the last glass of tokay.

"Fun!—what's his name?—Karamzin, right." He wiped his forehead with his hand. "Right, Karamzin—the great Karamzin. He's actually a Great Russian—but that doesn't matter—the great Karamzin! What is it he says? Don't you know?"

He grasped his hair as if he wanted to rummage around in his head.

"Right, right.

"All the wisdom of my life
Teaches me just this
Do not hope that love will last:
It's fleeting as a kiss

Faithfulness is but a joke.
Others change like fashion.
If you change yourself, my friend,
Don't expect compassion.

Hymen's trap therefore avoid.
Spouses are maltreated.
Love and cheat on all of them,
Else it's you who's cheated.

"It's really true.

"Spouses are maltreated.
Love and cheat on all of them,
Else it's you who's cheated.

"If you wanted, I could tell you about all my adventures.

"All women are mine, all of them: peasant women, Jewish women, middle-class, and noble women, all of them! Redheads, blondes, brunettes, black-haired women, all of them, all of them!

"Adventures, I'm telling you, nothing but adventures. For example which one, now? For example, I have a relationship now with a young married woman. Is she in love! — She's a lady, a lady from head to foot.

"But my head hurts a bit.

"I have another lover now. She is the wife of a bandit. Her husband was hanged, she herself—oh, I don't know. It doesn't matter to me anyway. — She can't even read. We don't talk with each other very much either, but we make love—like wolves!

"You need ten women all at once, or at least three: one for the bed, one, for the mind, and one for the heart—no, what am I saying. The heart plays no role, I'm telling you, no role at all."

He laughed in a childlike fashion and showed his magnificent white teeth.

"What do you need a heart for anyway? A man needs his heart for his children, his friends, his fatherland—but for a woman! Ha! ha! I've never again been betrayed by a woman since I've started to cheat on all of them. A funny comedy! You have to show them the man in you. Ha! ha! And how they love me since I've started only playing with them. I've made them all cry, all of them!"

"And how is your relationship to your wife," I asked, after he'd been silent for a long while.

"Well, we behave when we're together," he answered. "Sometimes when I—when I think back—to the time—think of her—I—I—get a headache—headache—but now we're having fun! Fun! Fun!"

He threw the wine bottle against the wall with the result that the Jew woke up with a start and tore down the prayer straps over his nose.

"So! Now I feel good!" he said and opened up his jacket. "Good. Fun!

"That's the way life is. When we're like this—then we feel good. Fun! Fun!"

He stood up in the middle of the bar, his arms coquettishly propped on his hips, and began to dance the Cossack while singing its innocently wild, intoxicatingly melancholy tune to accompany himself.

One moment he'd be sitting on the floor and kicking his legs out as if he were throwing away something superfluous; the next moment he'd jump up to the ceiling and whirl around in the air.

Then he stood still, his arms crossed on his chest, and shook his head most sadly. He grabbed it with his hand as if he wanted to tear it off, and shouted triumphantly like an eagle flying in the sun.

Suddenly the door was torn open, and there entered a venerable peasant with long white hair and doleful eyes, wearing a brown sierak.[24]

It was Simon Ostrov, the judge.

A melancholy smile crossed his pale face when he saw us.

"Sirs, how long have you been here?" he asked good-naturedly. "A long time, I'll bet. Well, I can't do anything about that now."

"So can we go?" asked the boyar.

"Of course," said Simon the judge.

"It really is too late," the other continued. "I mean for me. But you, perhaps. God be with you. Stay healthy."

He cheerfully stroked the Jewish woman's chin, and her whole face blushed.

He left and returned again. He squeezed my hand.

"Oh, well," he shouted, "water comes together with water and people with people."[25]

I stood at the threshold as he drove away. He waved one more time and then was gone.

I turned to the Jew.

"Oh, he's a jolly man," he moaned. "A dangerous man. They call him the Don Juan of Kolomea."

NOTES

1. District and district capital in eastern Galicia. Kolomea is derived from Colonia, for the current district capital rises upon the classical soil of a former Roman satellite city.

2. German (Swabian) village near Kolomea.

3. Swabian, a resident of Swabia in southwestern Germany, was the colloquial term for all Germans in Austrian Galicia (translator's note).

4. The whole of eastern Galicia, beginning with the San River, is home primarily to three million Little Russians who belong to the Greek Uniate Church and who form along with the population of southern Russia and the Cossacks a great nation of approximately 20 million. The beauty of their builds, the nobility of their facial features, their intellectual gifts, the harmony of their language, and the richness of their folk poetry confers upon them the greatest distinction among the Slavic tribes.

5. The instinct for self-help and self-government, which the southern Russians have enjoyed more than any other European peoples since ancient times, has created in Russia a downright communist or socialist peasant community; in Galicia, where it is called the *gromada*, it is more democratic. The peasant patrol, a kind of national guard, was officially recognized by the Austrian government in 1846 and was entrusted in the criminal code with

the right to use weapons in the same instances as the imperial troops and the gendarmerie. Since the Little Russians oppose the Poles and their ambitions, all security arrangements on the flatland were placed in the hands of the peasant patrol during all the Polish revolutions—with brilliant success. That was also the case in 1863, when our story takes place.

6. A derogatory nickname for "Jew."

7. The Kohlhaas of the east Slavic world in grand style. Chmielnicki, a Little Russian nobleman, robbed of his land, his wife, and his property by the Polish *starost*, incited the Cossacks to wage war against the Poles after he had vainly sought justice from the Polish crown. He repeatedly led their armies with great success into the heart of the country, which was completely devastated and plundered each time by his hordes.

8. *padam do nog*—I fall at your feet—Little Russian and Polish greeting.

9. The Little Russian nobles, also transplanted to Wallachia and the Moldau region, where their princes ruled for a long time.

10. All princes of the Little Russians before their union with Poland.

11. Wildly graceful national dance of the Little Russians.

12. A light, open coach.

13. At Easter, every house in Galicia has a "blessed meal" for relative, friends, and acquaintances, an open table with, among other things, national dishes that have all been blessed in the kitchen in advance.

14. Get out—march!

15. A booming independent mercantile city on the Russian border, mostly inhabited by Jews.

16. Every great house has its Jewish buyer, its factotum, its family Jew, who is called a "factor."

17. Starost, an official of the Polish crown who administered a district analogous to the Austrian administrative units, for which reason his title has been transferred to the Austrian governor.

18. Woman's jacket.

19. A Galician children's song.

20. Old Russian epic poem about the campaign of the Russian prince Igor against the Polovetsians. Distinguished by the power and the vividness of the narrative.

21. The time in Galicia when the landed gentry assembles in the district towns and the capital to sell their agricultural products—usually in advance—to the dealers, mostly Jews.

22. Bag.

23. A poetic form peculiar to the Little Russian folk song; of elegiac character and gripping, melancholy melody.

24. Long peasant coat with a hood, made of an unshorn pelt.

25. Little Russian proverb.

The Man Who Re-Enlisted

> Love is not love
> Which alters when it alteration finds,
> Or bends with the remover to remove.
>
> Shakespeare, Sonnet 116

Anyone who has floated upon the quiet sea in a light gondola, the plaything of the watery element, watched the indistinctly drawn shores of terra firma and the islands sink behind him, and, filled with foreboding, has seen in the sky above him a second sea with billowing clouds—that man will, perhaps, understand me when I tell about the Galician plain, the wintery ocean of snow, and a ride in a fleeting sleigh. The ocean and the plain both exert a melancholy attraction on the human soul. But flying in a sleigh is faster, more eaglelike—whereas the vessel in the water rocks like a duck in the air. The color of the endless plain and its melody are more serious, darker, more threatening; you see nature stripped bare, the struggle for existence; you feel death closer and sense its atmosphere; you hear its voices.

The bright winter afternoon had lured me out. I had decided to ride, but my sorrel was sick, and not every horse runs well in the snow. I had Mausche Leb Kattun, a great coachman in the sight of the Lord, hitch up his reliable horses to my sleigh. The day was magnificent, the air was still, as was the light, and the golden waves of the sun didn't tremble in the light breath of the earth. Air and light were one element. In the village, too, everything was still, no sound betrayed the residents of the silent straw huts; only the sparrows flew up screaming in flocks from along the fences.

Further off in the distance stood a small sleigh hitched to a small, limping horse no bigger than a foal. A peasant was using it to transport wood out of the forest. His half-grown girl was calling him and wading through the deep snow in her bare feet to pick up a small log that he had lost.

As we flew down the bare mountain to the sound of bright, ringing bells, the plain lay before us, immeasurable, incomprehensible, and infinite. The wintery ermine cloaked it in supreme majesty. It was completely covered in snow; only the bare trunks of the low-growing willows, the long-armed country wells further off, and away in the distance, a few rust-colored stray huts made black dots on the snowy white fur.

Mausche Leb Kattun roused himself and shouted. His first view of the plain worked on him like a fast poison. His Palestinian imagination began speaking in biblical phrases, and with a single beat of its wings, it left the region of furred animals for that of palms and cedars. He was tossed around on his seat like a sick man with a fever; he rooted around in his brain to find a thousand images for the incomprehensibility that tormented him; he spat out allegories by the dozen until I told him to be silent. Then he just muttered to himself. I don't know whether he was continuing the conversation with himself or whether he was praying. Did he find the right analogy in the end? Perhaps an infinite piece of white paper on which he wrote his infinite calculations and counted, counted.

We flew down the firm path.

There was a farm off to one side and a tiny village behind it; the snow had turned everything to silver; the miserable, overhanging roofs were covered with silver, the little window panes with silver blossoms; every gutter, every fountain, every deformed fruit tree was hung with silver tassels. High walls surrounded every dwelling. People had dug pathways like a dachshund or a fox does. The light smoke rising from the roofs seemed to freeze in the air. Great, silver poplars stood around the farm. Here and there little motes of frost fluttered up like swarms of diamond mosquitos and floated through the air—a miniature thunderstorm—firing off thousands of small flashes.

At the far end of the little hamlet, peasant boys with white heads and red cheeks were chasing each other, half-naked in the snow. They made a snowman, and in his wide mouth they had stuck a long pipe like the noblemen smoke. A young peasant was sitting there on a hand sled, and a couple of pretty girls with long, brown braids and puffy white blouses were pulling him through every topography imaginable. Their high spirits soared above them like a jubilant lark. How they laughed! And he laughed even more wildly and lost his cap.

We flew past the forest.

Where is its melody? The fox yelps hoarsely and the jackdaw cries. The colorful red leaves overhead are uniformly encased in snow. A rosy, damp aroma flows around the forest and the sky. Before us there lie only a few snowy hills, like the frozen waves of a white sea. Wherever the white sky sinks into it, there is a spot of brilliance, but only an eye looking into the sun can see it. The village and the red forest sink behind us; the last peaks of the bare mountains light up one more time, and then they, too, sink like the hills and the sparse trees. The boundless plain has received us. There is nothing but snow before and behind us; the white sky above us is like snow; we are surrounded by the deepest solitude, by death and silence.

We glide along like in a dream. The horses seem to swim in the snow, and the sleigh follows noiselessly. Off to the side, a little gray mouse runs across the field of snow. There is no chimney, no hollow tree trunk, no molehill to be seen far and wide, and yet it is running so carefully and purposefully. Where to? By now it's just a small, dark dot. Then the solitude surrounds us again. It seems that we've made no progress. Nothing changes in front or behind us, not even the sky. It stands immobile, cloudless, monotonous, as if freshly whitewashed; it doesn't move; it doesn't even shimmer. Only the air reveals the evening ever more clearly, and it becomes sharper, cutting like glass.

Mausche Kattun had just cut himself. In shock, he grabbed some snow, rubbed his ear, and then pulled the flap of his hat over his ear. Finally, our sleigh was standing like a vessel in the quiet sea that moves without leaving the spot. We only think we are traveling, nothing behind us and nothing in front of us, just as we believe we are living. For are we living? Doesn't living mean being? And doesn't no longer being mean never having been?

A raven flies past; it sails mightily with its black pinions, silent, its beak open. Then it glides around a hill of snow. Is it a gravel pile or a lost and sunken haystack in which it sniffs a mouse? Neither. Half flying and half hopping, it circles the hill, limping while flying and fluttering while walking, looks at it from all sides, takes its stand on top of the hill, and starts hacking into it. It is carrion. And there's the wolf already with its shaggy nape; it lifts its snout and draws air; then it trots on over. When it gets there, it starts sniffing, too, looks at the bird, grovels and wags its tail like a dog that's just found its master again. The raven stands up top, hoarse but lively, and beats its wings. "Come, brother, there's enough for both of us." And they laugh at each other, the rascals.

In sinking, the sun gradually becomes visible low on the horizon as a dazzling ball of haze. It doesn't set, it sinks into the snow, which, in turn, dissolves and flows like molten gold; waves of gold play at our feet and wondrous colors run across the snow, which is sprinkled with liquid silver. Then it is extinguished. The thousand lights that it cast forth run together and turn pale. A light, red aura still floats in the air, and then it dissolves as well. Everything is colorless again, cold and immobile.

It was just for a moment.

The wind from the east suddenly collides into us sharply and icily.

In the distance, a sleigh swims past, and the fleeting waves of air carry the whimpering sound of its little bell over to us; then it is engulfed by the ashen-colored fog that quickly rises on the horizon, rolls into a ball, and surges like the sea. It quickly becomes dark, and formless, gray-white clouds cover the sky, a terrible armada, sail after sail. Then the wind strikes at them, blows them up and they swim closer; they approach us as we ride into them. Evening mists blaze forth and dissolve into light shadows.

The Jew brings his horses to a stop.

"There's a storm coming," he says with a worried face. "We could be overcome by snowdrifts. Tulava is closer than heading back. What do you think, sir?"

"We'll go to Tulava."

He cracks his whip twice over the heads of his animals.

We fly onward. Scraps of fog whiz around us like birds with great, dull wings. There's the sacred image on the stone column; that's where the road to Tulava turns to the right.

The wind immediately beats into the back of our necks with both fists; it howls with a horrifying, wretched voice; from above, it plunges down into the snow, churns it up, shatters the large clouds, throws them back to earth in feathery clumps and threatens to cover us over. The horses put their heads between their legs and snort. The storm drives whirling white columns up into the heavens, sweeps the plain with white brooms, gathering everything into monstrous piles with which it buries people, animals, and whole villages.

The air burns as if aglow. It has become solid and, shattered by the storm, flies around in pieces and forces its way into the lungs like splinters of glass when you breathe.

The horses make only slow progress; they are being buried by the snow, the air, and the wind.

The snow has become an element in which we swim with all our might so as not to drown; an element that we breathe and that threatens to burn us alive. In the midst of the most terrifying movement, nature has become rigid and icy. We ourselves are only fragments of the all-encompassing cold and rigor. You understand how the ice keeps the world buried, how you stop living without dying or decaying. Monstrous elephants, gigantic mammoths, lie uncorrupted in it, stored away for the soup pots of ambitious scholars. You think of primeval dinner parties and laugh. In fact, you are overcome with the desire to laugh. Tickling, after all, stimulates you to laugh, and the cold tickles terribly, uninterruptedly, cruelly. People who only appear to be dead sneeze when they are tickled and then come back to life.

Everything is frozen. Thoughts lie on the brain like icicles, the soul gets an icy cover, and the blood falls like mercury. You no longer think your thoughts; you no longer feel like other men feel; morality and Christianity hang in our hair like congealed fog; that part of us that belongs to the elements is violently turned outward. We sometimes become so angry when a nail won't go into the wall that we smash its metal head with one blow. We throw a narrow boot into the corner and smother it with the most remarkable curses. Here, the struggle is for existence, but you fight it like an element yourself, patiently, silently, resigned, almost apathetically.

The life that we so love has become paralyzed. We are a stone or a piece of ice, just one more frozen bubble in the struggle of the elements.

You watch your own pulse as if it were a stranger's. A white curtain separates us from our horses; the sleigh carries us through the storm like a boat without a rudder, without sails—it's almost standing still.

The hurricane continues its monotonous howl, the air burns, and the snow whirls. Space and time disappear. Are we moving forward? Are we standing still? Is it night or is it day?

Slowly the clouds drift off to the west. The horses begin to whinny again; then they become visible again, their backs covered with snow. Thick flakes are falling, and the earth is covered with several feet of them, but you can see again and can move forward. The storm is only panting now and rolling around in the snow with a whimper. The fog is lying on the ground like gray-colored debris. Where are we?

Around us, everything has been drifted over; there is no road and no pile of stones or wooden cross to point the way toward it. The horses are wading up to their chests. Only in the distance are there still some isolated, lost sounds from the storm. We stop, then move forward again. The Jew sweeps his animals' backs with the handle of his whip. Two ravens fly past, soundlessly, barely moving their black wings. The falling snow devours them. The horses shake themselves and go faster. Only light, watery flakes are falling now. But in the distance, everything is still enveloped. Again we stop and consult with one another.

The night falls; gloomy, cloudy twilight spreads out and wraps itself around us more and more. The Jew whips the horses, and they throw their legs out in front of themselves at a faster and faster pace. A glowing red strip is lying on the horizon. We turn towards it. It seems as if the red moon had fallen onto the earth and was lying there in the snow, extinguishing itself. Then it flares up and illuminates the stark, black shadows.

"It's the peasant patrol by the little birch wood," the Jew says, "and Tulava lies on the other side of the wood."

As we approached, the little birch wood arose in front of us like a dark wall, garishly illuminated in places by the monstrous fire that the peasant patrol was industriously keeping alive at its edge. The fire lay in a half-circle towards the forest so that the wind, which thrust against the small birches here and there, would drive the flames outward. The smoke slowly drifted towards the forest, where it hung from the trees in pieces and then softly floated off.

A warm, bright haze lay around the fire. The people who were holding watch there looked like shadows in it. The Jew waved to them.

They immediately sank from view again. Only one of them approached us.

"It's Balaban," Leb Kattun said. "Don't you know him? He's the capitulant."[1]

He was a former soldier, the watchman of the village of Tulava, a highly respected, conscientious man in this area. I had heard of him more than once, but had had no opportunity up until now of getting to know him; I therefore observed him with some interest. His tall build and his bearing, his head, his free, rhythmic movements immediately gave me a definite impression of strength. His greeting was polite, but not subservient.

"Did the storm do any damage to you?" he asked and looked at the horses. "I hope the driver did his best."

Just like a gentleman giving you lodging, applying equal amounts of grace and dignity. With an aristocratic sweep of the hand, he invited me over to the fire. "The horses are tired and sweating," he said, "and then there's the darkness. You'll have to rest."

"And that's just what we want to do," I replied, for I was attracted by the conviviality of the fire and by the capitulant. As he was leading the way, a boy came running up.

He gently passed his hand over the boy's white-blond head. And he was transformed. I saw that he was a man whom you didn't understand completely with one glance.

The people around the fire stood up.

"Well, what are you all doing here?" I said.

They all looked at the capitulant.

"The nearby estate owners," he said seriously, "and probably other Poles as well, are heading to Tulava today. They're sure to have emissaries[2] and documents and be making plans there. Some of them show up without a pass. So we have to do our duty. Perhaps we can discover something. That's the whole story."

"Yes, we're keeping watch," said the boy.

"In this storm?" I cried.

"Well, we do what's expected of us," the capitulant answered, "and if we overlook them in this blizzard, at least we were here."

So he didn't even understand that the battle of the elements or the danger involved could stop him from doing what he considered to be his duty. That was remarkable.

He took the horses by the mane and led the sleigh over to the fire, took out a blanket, and spread it out for me.

"The ground is dry," he assured me. "We've been lying here since this morning and keeping a fire that you could roast an ox over."

Indeed, the ashes lay around it for several paces and it was quite warm. The flames stood upright or shot out from the circle in which we were arranged. The snowflakes came like silver moths and sank with lowered wings into the embers.

"They're coming from Zavala, too," the boy noted.

"Of course. All the beautiful women like making revolutions," I said.

"Is she coming, too, the lady?" the Jew asked, and his fingers drummed on the capitulant's shoulder.

"How would I know," he said and moved his head like a horse trying to shoo a bothersome fly away. For a moment, something concealed and extraordinary flickered in his eye while his face remained unchanged. Then he stared into the smoke that was drifting toward the birches.

It was quite still; only the wind blew softly into the fire. I lay down on my side and looked at the people.

I knew the peasant who was standing watch with his scythe at the corner of the forest and who returned to the group from time to time, more to hear what the people around the fire were saying than to warm himself. His name was Mrak, and he had the decisive, serious face that you usually see on our peasants.

Another one, who was squatting down near the fire closest to me, was a stranger to me. He was a morose type in a furry, mouse-colored serak;[3] his pyramidal head, pointed on top and broad down below, was wearing a small cap made of dirty white sheepskin. When I looked at him from the side, he seemed to me to be badly cut out from shabby, old, gray cardboard. His nose was especially long and pointed, thin and feltlike. His mouth had stayed caught in the scissors, and his chin seemed lost in his neck. Even the wrinkles of his colorless face were clumsy. The whole person seemed malformed. The fire exaggerated his silhouette and cast it against the snow in an irresistibly comical fashion.

Next to him, lying flat on his stomach, was a man whom the poodle-blond boy, named Jur, called Cousin Mongol. There's a battlefield in the vicinity on which a Tartar horde suffered a bloody loss two hundred years ago. Ruined villages were repopulated with the prisoners the locals had taken. I can safely bet that our Mongol had his beginnings there. He's not half as tall as our cardboard man when he's fully stretched out, but this little pot stands firmly on the ground. The uncovered back of his neck bursts with strength. He's lying there in linen breeches and an open, linen shirt, his bare chest on the hot ashes and his naked legs in the snow. Everything about Cousin Mongol is shoddy work as well. How did they ever shove this mighty chest and these broad hips together in one piece? And his face, or what he presents to the world as a face! They made a pair of miserable little holes for his lively, dark eyes, but as if to make up for that, the skin near the mouth makes the most abhorrent wrinkles. The eyes are slit steeply downward, and the nose points up with such nostrils that one of them would be big enough for both his eyes. And then he's as yellow as envy personified in a folk-play, and he pulls his knitted cap down over his thin, wiry black hair until it meets his long pointy ears.

The main person there was clearly the capitulant, Frinko Balaban.

How old was he? Who could be sure? But he was a man.

A man who couldn't be overlooked—neither in physical stature nor in the community, such as here at the peasant patrol's fire. An earthen brown coat tied with a black lacquered belt clothed his slender and powerful build. He had buttoned it shut all the way to the top, a faded, old cloth wrapped around his neck, and was wearing a pair of worn out blue soldier's pants over his boots, city fashion. At his waist hung his tobacco pouch, made out of a pig's bladder, which he used when stuffing his pipe, and a large knife. The others were armed with scythes and flails, but he had a single-barreled flintlock laid across his knee. Next to his two service awards, he had a third ribbon pinned to his chest. The tall, round sheepskin cap lent his fine head the dignity of a rabbi and the wildness of a janissary; it helped his tightly cut brown hair frame a remarkable face, a face with gentle lines, a fine nose and mouth, covered, by virtue of the time he spent in the field, with that beautiful bronze that, with the two melancholy lines of the mouth and the drooping mustache, gives our soldier his typical character. But his honest eye was so sunken under his firm brows, so damp that it seemed filled with tears, and it was painful to see it, even though his gaze was calm. That's what it was, that and the voice. The whole man was so firm and soldierlike, and yet everything in him sounded broken. The sounds came from his chest in pieces, and his manner of speaking had something monotonous and solemn about it. So might the Christian martyrs have spoken at the stake or on the hot sands of the arena.

They also had a dog by the fire, an ordinary peasant dog of indeterminate color, with a collar of dark hair and the pretty head of a fox. He was sleeping in the warm ashes, his pointy snout bedded on his front paws, and just quietly moved his tail when the capitulant's melancholy voice struck his ear.

Everyone in the watch spoke softly and seriously; only the Jew chattered.

"I know a woman for you," he was teasing the discharged soldier, "a pretty widow. I know that's important to you, really pretty and a big estate, which is pretty too. What do you think? She's already been asking about you."

He looked around at each man in the circle, one after the other, but no one paid him any attention. That seemed to make Leb Kattun really get talkative. He brushed Balaban's back off with his hand and cried: "God, the Just! You don't want a wife!"

He squinted with one eye and shot a cute look at the peasants.

"He's sworn it. A man like him! He's sworn he'll take no wife!"

The capitulant looked over his shoulder at him in such a way that the Jew coughed, went back to the sleigh, and sat down with his back to the peasants. He swung his legs back and forth for a while, calculated, prayed, and finally fell asleep. While he was knocking his heels rhythmically against the wood, he woke the dog up.

"Quiet, Polack!" the boy said to the dog.

The foxlike head turned to the capitulant, and when he remained silent, the dog stood up and walked over to me, stretching out his rear feet behind him, sniffed at me, walked over to the sleigh, and sniffed the horses. They lowered their heads towards him, and he raised his snout toward them, licked the frozen haze from their mouths, wagged his tail, and whimpered in a friendly fashion. Then he lifted his nose, walked solemnly over to the Jew, sniffed him, turned immediately around, and lifted his leg. Then he encountered the cold air, sneezed, and retreated quickly to the fire where he buried his nose in the warm ashes.

"There's a man over there, running across the snow," suddenly cried the peasant who was keeping watch at the corner of the forest. We all looked in the direction he was pointing; only the capitulant remained quietly seated.

"Who else is it going to be?" he said calmly, turned his head slightly toward the running figure, and smiled. "Don't you know who it is?"

"Ah, it's Kolanko," the cardboard man reassured us in a whiny tone. As he did so, he scratched himself behind the ear and looked very unhappy."

"He's all we needed," Jur, the boy, said with a smart lip and importantly crossed his arms over his chest.

The capitulant made a dismissive gesture by moving his flat hand downwards and turned to me at the same time

"You must know, sir," he said seriously, "that he is more than a hundred years old, a strange man, an experienced man, a smart man, just a bit talkative, even childish now; he laughs without cause and even cries without cause. As childish as people usually are when they're a hundred years old."

And there he was in person, relieving the capitulant of any further necessity for explanation, a small, quick man with unsteady legs and trembling arms, a sunken chest, a dried-out yellow throat, and an ancient little yellow face in which there was no life except for the eyes, which had sunk deeply into their sockets, the better to penetrate and soak up everything they encountered.

He was wearing a solid pair of boots, warm leggings, a long, greasy sheepskin, a cap made from a three-colored cat skin, and was holding a red-striped feather cushion in his arms as if it were a child, and he spoke so rapidly with his toothless mouth that you couldn't always understand him.

"I've got you, you slippery eels!" he shouted, giggling at first and then complaining about something that escaped me; later I heard him praising the capitulant.

He sat down near him and spent some time looking into everyone's face, one after the other, in the order in which we were sitting around the fire, until he came to me, whereupon he stretched out his little, shrunken neck, raised his eyebrows, stood up, bowed three times, and sat back down again.

"The gentleman won't know what to make of me," he giggled and again swallowed a few words. "You see, I'm an old man who's watched everybody close to him die. As you see me now, I'm as alone as a child in its mother's belly. Last year I still had a raven, and I thought it would grow old with me, but something got it in the wing. Now there's no one in my hut but me. Who wants to stay with an old man? — And then I don't sleep, either. That's one of those things when you're old. You think of a lot of things. I'm scared when I'm alone at night, it's true." He laughed in such a way that the air whistled through his nose. "The fog grows hands and the snow feet at night, and the moon takes on a face and eyes, big eyes like a crazy person's, and it asks all kinds of things, the fool, that people like us can't answer!"

He spat mightily.

"You see, I sneak away whenever I want, my good sir, and run to wherever I know our people are."

The old man was entertaining me.

"You like being out with people?" I asked.

"Actually, there's a lot of things about it that bore me."

The cardboard man gave him an indignant look.

"Well, I'm not going to say anything," Kolanko continued. "But there's nothing I haven't heard already. I know everything. Everything. And even if there is something new there, what does it matter that Ivan did something dumber than Basyl when he tried to seduce his friend's wife. Don't bother me with those things. You're all such greenhorns. The capitulant is the only one still worth listening to, and that's why I came running over to your fire."

"So life bores you," I said with some curiosity.

"Indeed."

"And are you looking forward to death?"

"Real death? Yes."

"What do you mean by real death?"

"A death, sir, that makes a living man dead for ever, but not that he lies in the ground for a while and then can put his limbs together again and start all over."

"He fears eternal life," the cardboard man said, nodding his head toward me.

We all looked at the old man. I was eager to hear him, for our peasants, without ever having seen a book or having made a stroke with a pen, are born politicians and philosophers. They have the wisdom of the Orient in them like the poor fishermen, shepherds, and beggars in the thousand and one nights that Harun al-Rashid spent time with. I expected to hear things that you don't hear everyday and that you can read neither in Hegel nor in Moleschott.

"What do you actually get out of this life?" the old man asked quietly and distinctly. "You greenhorns, you keep hoping to live on and on. Somebody like me, who's seen everything, suffered everything that a man can suffer"—he sank into thought.

"Eternal life would really have to be terribly boring," he said after a while, "but I know something that would be even more terrible."

"What would that be?"

"To be born again." He laughed out loud.

"That never occurred to me before," the cardboard man said thoughtfully. "The old man is right."

The capitulant stared into the fire with glassy eyes like a man frozen. The old man poked him with his elbow.

"Well, what do you think?"

"God save me," the capitulant said. "I don't want to be born again."

"You see, young master," the old man began again," this is the way I see it: you're bored enough with your hundred years under your belt, but it will come to an end some day. But if you start getting bored with eternal life, there's no way out. Let's assume, people, that everything they say about heaven is really so. Okay. In the beginning, sir, everything would be pleasant, so to speak; there'd be no lack of pleasant conversations—Saint Sebastian would tell me how the Turks shot at him with feathered arrows and nailed him up like an owl, and how he wasn't quite dead yet, and how a widow saved him and took him into her house, and how he then walked right up to that pagan emperor and said, 'You dog!' and then was beaten to death again. Then the holy Bishop Polycarp would tell me about the clever answer that he gave a pagan, some Roman field marshal lieutenant or something, and how he was then baked at the stake, and Saint Vincent would describe to me how he was made to lie down on sharp splinters of glass. But it would end up with Saint Sebastian telling me about the arrows for the thousandth time, and Saint Vincent and his sharp splinters for the thousandth time and then—not to be able to sleep! In sleep man is at least dead for a little while. And then you can yawn, too, but the devil knows whether pure spirits can yawn."

"You're pretty chipper," I said. "Do you think you'll live much past a hundred."

"Yes, unfortunately," he replied. "When you've seen what this life is like for a hundred years, sir, you've had enough. You'd like to sleep for a long, long time, and if it were possible, never wake up again."

He sank in thought and rocked his feather cushion back and forth in front of him. "Heaven, sir, can't be anything but a bad joke. You see, down here, every living thing, whether animal or man, has to run around like crazy just to stay alive; one thing murders the next, and this one lives from that one, and up there all those lazy people need to be fed. If there is eternal life, sir, it's going to mean working and doing without and suffering all over again. Instead of 'protect us from evil,' you should pray 'protect us from life.'"

"Don't you believe in a second life?" the capitulant asked, his voice trembling at the question.

"I'm not saying anything about that," Kolanko replied, digging around in his nose. "Holy Scripture, however, is a book that God himself wrote. The deacon is sure to know. The deacon says that there are places in there where you can say that God himself didn't know back then if he'd succeeded in making man's soul immortal. It's written there: Man's lot is the same as the animals; as they die, so does he; and they all have the same breath, and man has no more than the animals. Well, you see, our dear Lord will certainly know what he's talking about. And it is also written: All things go to the same place; everything is made of dust and will turn to dust again. Who knows if man's spirit rises upwards and the animals' breath goes down under the earth? And so I saw that there is nothing better for man than to be happy in his work; that is his lot, for who shall bring him to the point that he can see what will happen when he is gone. That's what it says, word for word."

"Nothing better for man than that he be happy in his work," the capitulant cried. "You have to fulfill your obligations. That's the best. What else could you want on this earth?"

For the time being, the old man occupied my attention more than the capitulant.

"Listen, friend," I turned to him. "Is it true, then, that you want to die forever, and that death doesn't cause you the least fear?"

"Oh, it does, it does, young sir," he nodded with a giggle. "I'm really terrified of death."

"I don't understand."

"Well, for example; when I'm alive, I at least have the hope that it will all end someday; isn't that so?"

It seemed to me that he was looking right down into the depths of my soul with his little gray eyes.

"But when death comes, this moment that I've been waiting for so hard for a hundred years, and I end up going on living— then I'd really be stuck." The whole circle laughed.

"I beg you, sir," the old man quickly continued, "look at me. I'm not a desperate man, a failed peasant maybe or some incompetent writer; but life is tedious to me, really quite disgusting. You know, that's a discovery that everyone would make soon enough if he'd only do himself the small favor of thinking about himself. When people find a suicide, hanged, for example, they're amazed —'How could that have happened?'—What are they talking about? Things just didn't work out for him."

It was quite still for a moment. The fire did its work, and the smoke rolled lazily toward the birch forest. The wind had let up.

The hundred-year-old man looked at the capitulant.

"He's one of them," he said quietly. "Isn't he?"

The capitulant's head had sunk down on his chest. He was silent.

"But tell us a story, Balaban."

"Tell us something, friend," I said. "They say that you are a good storyteller."

The capitulant laughed bleakly.

"Should I tell you a fairy tale?" he asked obligingly.

"No, something you've experienced yourself."

The old man nodded approvingly.

"Yes, he knows more than many other men."

The capitulant ran his hand gently over his forehead.

"What should I tell you about?"

The cardboard man stuck his neck out as far as he could and blinked in irritation with his tiny eyes.

"What was the Jew talking about before?" he asked.

"Oh, just a story," the capitulant said quietly. His gaze sank into the fire, and a quiet, ineffably moving sadness settled upon his features.

"A story?" asked Kolanko eagerly.

"Well, a story like many others," the capitulant murmured.

"I see," said the old man.

"An old story, and not very entertaining."

"It's a love story," the cardboard man added softly and shyly, looking up from below at the former soldier as if afraid.

"It's sure to be something curious," Kolanko cried.

"It's nothing curious, either," the capitulant said. "Something that you encounter every day. I'll—especially because the gentleman is here—it'll be better if I tell you about the Hungarian war. We were marching—"

"You're not going to make us march from Dukla to Kashau again, are you?" the old man interrupted him. "This would be the seventh time, I think. You might tell us something different."

"Just tell the story," said the cardboard man.

"What story?"

"The one about Katharina von Baran from over there, about the mistress of the estate," the cardboard man said, not really loudly, but with a kind of bitter contempt, and at the same time, something of the enmity of our peasants toward the aristocracy flamed up in his eye.

"Did you all know her?" the capitulant asked without looking up.

No one dared speak.

"I knew her."

His voice trembled as sadly as the last note of our folk songs. He slowly raised his head, and his eyes were wide open, calm, and visionary in his pale face.

"He'll tell us about it now," the Mongol whispered and poked the cardboard man gently in the side.

Everyone settled down to listen to him in comfort. Mrak, who was marching back and forth like a genuine guard, came to a stop and leaned on his scythe.

"Let me see: what were things like when I first saw her?" the capitulant began. "Right, it was in the alder bushes near Tulava; she was looking for hazelnuts and had gotten a thorn, a long, sharp thorn, you know, in her foot. So she was sitting there at the edge of the bushes and crying, and when I saw the pretty girl sitting there, crying so bitterly, I felt sorry for her. So I stopped and asked, 'What's the matter?'

"She didn't answer, but only tugged at the thorn and sobbed still harder. Then I noticed what my little bird's problem was, squatted down next to her, and said: 'Wait, I'll help you.' She stopped crying, gave me her foot without a moment's hesitation, and blinked while looking sideways at me. I got hold of it immediately, the thorn, you know, and when I pulled it out, she just hissed a little bit through her teeth. Then she tore her scarf down over her face, jumped up, and ran off without saying thanks.

"After that, whenever she saw me, even from a distance, she ran from me like from a haydamak. And I was always glad to find her.

"Once I was coming back from the market with a heavily loaded cart and was walking next to the horses, and she was standing behind a fence, and when I noticed her, she quickly ducked and flashed her dark eyes through the willow branches at me like a cat.

"'Why are you hiding, Katharina?' I cried. 'I won't hurt you.' I brought the horses to a stop.

"But the girl remained silent.

"'What have you gotten into your head that you're always running away? I'm not chasing you.'

"Then she showed herself again, held her arm in front of her eyes, and smiled, the rascal. Oh, what a pretty little mouth she had and her teeth, like white coral!

"'You're coming from the fair, Balaban,' she said with embarrassment.

"'That's right, Katharina,' I answered politely.

"'Oh, if only I could run around the world like you do,' she said.

"'Where would you go, Katharina?'

"'To the fair, I think, and I'd have to see all the cities and the Black Sea, but Kolomea first of all,' she answered me.

"'Haven't you been to Kolomea?' I asked.

"'Never.'

"'Never?'

"'I've never seen any city,' she continued and looked at me with a little more courage. 'Is it true that two or three houses are stacked up on top of each other there? And the nobles travel around in boxes? That have four wheels? And there's a house full of soldiers?'

"I explained all of that to her, and she asked all kinds of funny things; she didn't know any better back then. I had to laugh; such nonsense! By God! She looked at me with fright and then quickly hid her head under her arm again, like a chicken. The sun was just going down; I can still see it all quite clearly, the street, the fence, the pretty girl. The sky behind her was like a burning red cloth all spread out. I couldn't even look in her direction. With one hand, I turned the cart around and with the other, I dragged the handle of my whip through the sand.

"The Sunday after that I met my Katharina—forgive me. I say my Katharina. Such a stupid habit. Well, I met her, in church, you see. I was praying nicely and only looked over toward her from time to time. When the people leave after mass, there's always an unbelievable crush around the holy water font, and I used my elbows to make my way through the crowd and brought my pretty Katharina the sanctified water in my cupped hand. She smiled, dipped her fingers in, made the sign of the cross, and then she sprinkled me with it, the rascal, and ran off.

"From that time on, I thought of her all the time, against my will. That was a misfortune. I really spent a lot of time trying to figure out where I could run into her so that it would seem as if she accidently crossed my path. Oh, my God, it's just a plain love story like any other.

"One day I was performing my mandatory service at the estate, and I ran into her coming out of the house. The master was lying in the window, like this, in his sleeping gown, you know, and smoking his chibouk. Katharina did something to keep herself busy nearby, and I didn't pay her any attention.

"'I'm leaving now, Balaban,' she said after a while.

"'Good, that you're leaving,' I said in a low voice. 'What are you doing in the estate house? There's not much that's good here for a pretty young thing like you.'

"Katharina turned red. I don't know if it was from anger or shame.

"'What does it matter to you?' she asked, kind of sideways.

"I became very embarrassed, really embarrassed.

"'What does it matter to me?' I then said in all seriousness. 'The devil plays his game everywhere, and I worry about every poor human soul that belongs to our Lord God.'

"'I'm just a poor girl,' she said. "Who's going to give me anything? Who will marry me? And yet I have to live, and the same things that make other women happy make me happy too. I'd like to earn something nice here at the estate, a new scarf for my head at least, or some of those lovely corals, or even a fur.'

"'What do you need corals for,' I said, 'or—'

"'Nobody is going to like me like this,' she cried.

"'Whoever said that would be lying,' I said heatedly.

"I was quite in love with the young thing, I'm telling you, and now I knew what I had to do. I thought of how in the old stories and songs the czar won the czarina and the fisherman got his wife by means of beautiful gifts, and I kept track of my groschen until the Feast of the Magi came.

"That evening, I was the first to paint myself black. I had gotten a red altar-cloth from the deacon and used it as a cloak, and I made a big, pointed crown out of gold paper. I was the black king, and I had dressed up two good friends, Ivan Stepnuk and Pazorek, as the two white kings, and my cousin Jusef, the one that was taken from us by the pox, was our servant, a real Moor.

"He really knew how to carry the presents. So we got on our way, the wise men from the Orient, and sang the usual song. Pazorek carried the star on a long pole.

"When we entered Katharina's house, the girls started running around screaming like a clutch of partridges, but the old man, her father, smiled and got the brandy down from the shelf in order to treat us hospitably. While the others were drinking with him, as is expected, I politely took Katharina by the hand, bowed, and said: 'I bless you, flower of the Occident. We Kings of the Orient, following the star that showed us the way to our Savior, entered this land where your beauty and honor came to our attention. We have entered your hut in order to bow to you and to bring you presents.'

"And with that I waved to my cousin Jusef, our black servant, took a big, beautiful, red scarf from his hands, and presented it to her, and then I pulled out three strands of big, beautiful, red coral beads and presented them to her as well. I had bought both things with my good money in Kolomea. My Katharina bent over with embarrassment, turned blood-red, and hid both her hands between her knees, but her eyes seemed to devour the scarf, not to mention the coral beads, and I gently pulled her down onto the bench by the oven and nicely laid my presents in her lap. Then we talked so prettily with each other. I said, 'Beautiful czarina, within a year I'll bring you a lovely fur made of sable pelts or white ermine, as you command,' and she said: 'Majestic King of the Moors, I'm not the daughter of the Czar, but just a poor peasant girl, and a sheepskin is enough for me.' To which I replied: 'You are as beautiful as the Czar's daughter, that is the honest truth. In our country it is a different world, a different people, and a different earth. Every man has a hundred wives and a king has a thousand, but I only know one woman that I would like for my whole life.'

"The others became more and more cheerful and were shouting, and Pazorek got up the nerve to lift my Katharina up off the bench and spun around with her like a top, but I sat quietly and watched them, and then my heart began to hurt so strangely. The whole world looked different to me, so strange. Just like there are people who lose their sight at night, I was suddenly blind in broad daylight; the world that I saw was not this world, our world; it was as if I was looking inside myself where I'd suddenly retrieved my nigh vision and saw strange apparitions in the bushes and the fields. In the air and water, in the moonlight, I saw things that no other man saw and heard what no one heard or felt—many, many years have passed since then, but I still haven't found the words to tell you what I felt that day. My heart grew so wide and then so narrow, flew one minute and stood still the next.—Oh, such stupidity.'

The capitulant smiled sadly and then slowly rocked his head from side to side.

"Two days after the Feast of the Magi, I ran into Katharina on her way somewhere.

"'Did you wash yourself with lye?' she shouted from afar and laughed knavishly.

"I wanted to catch her, but she escaped me this time as well.

"We started holding long conversations whenever we ran into each other, and I visited her in her hut. The neighbors were already starting to talk.

"'Do you know what people are saying?' I said to Katharina.

"'How should I know?'

"'They say that you're my lover.'

"'Isn't it true?' the poor child asked, her eyes opened wide. 'Didn't I get a scarf from you and coral beads?'

"I was quiet.

"People really were saying it, and everyone kept his distance. And it soon was true," the capitulant said quietly, and looked with embarrassment into the glowing ashes; his face displayed a calm glow, and his eyes seemed transparent and light from within.

I glanced at the peasants. Kolanko was listening with a furrowed brow and his lips pressed together. The cardboard man and Jur, who was sitting behind him, were leaning on each other like sheaves of hay. The Mongol was lying in the ashes like a fish on the sand, forgetting to breath from sheer tension and only gasping for air now and then.

"She was a good, pretty girl, this Katharina," the cardboard man whispered energetically to me, "and she turned into a real, proud woman, a genuine mistress. She has a way of walking, sir, like a czarina, and she's as beautiful as the devil."

"Is she still like that?"

"She certainly is."

"I kissed her hand once," the boy cried with his eyes aglow. "She pulled her glove down and let me kiss it, a hand like a high-born lady's, so white, so round—a fine little hand."

"She was a good, pretty girl," the capitulant repeated, "hard-working, cheerful. She sang while she worked and danced like a majka. She found an answer to everything you said and sometimes came up with thoughts like a witch's.

She was big rather than small and had brown hair and such good, blue eyes, eyes like twilight, you know; sometimes they'd be so astonished and shy, like an animal's. Her head was—so noble, is what I'd almost say. In the estate owner's garden there was an old woman made of stone; I mean a woman made of stone, one of the ancient goddesses. She had the same noble head, the same severe features. A beautiful woman and as cheerful as the water in the mountains in the summer. It was difficult not to love her. She was really the dearest soul to me in the world. I could talk to her like to my mother; I could tell her everything, confide everything to her; in her presence I had no fear, no shame, no arrogance. Sometimes she sat like a saint in the church, quiet and earnest, and I felt a solemnity, as if I should pray, and I confessed, so to speak, everything to her that was in my heart. She knew every corner of my soul; nothing in me was hidden from her or God. And she—she was like my child, like an animal that I had taken from its nest and raised. I only had to look at her and she already knew my thoughts and my wishes.

"It was as if my mother had bathed me in honey, the way she would kiss me all over and often bite me like a snake.

"I was happy." He smiled. "That is, when I think back on that now, I was happy then, but I didn't know it. But that it could ever be different—I truly couldn't imagine that.

"Well, I might as well tell you about it. Spring came again. I'd been noticing a change for some time. Katharina seemed to me to be carrying her head a bit high.

"One evening I was leading the horses to the watering trough. It was by the well behind the willows, you know. She let me wait. It was the first time that that had happened. And then suddenly there she was, coming across the meadow as delicate as a water thrush, swinging the pails on her shoulder and singing a happy song:

"I don't go in the church to pray,
I go to see my man.
I take a quick look at the priest,
And on my darling then I feast."

"She sang so cheerfully, as joyously as a lark, and I was so sad. I kissed her nicely and hugged her prettily, and didn't say anything cross to her, and she had nothing good to say to me. She just bent down and filled her pails, and I handed them to her, and she set then on her pole and then set them down again.

"'I don't know what's going to happen,' she began, playing in the water with the tips of her toes. 'I have to tell you that the estate owner is following me around.'

"'The estate owner?' I said, almost in shock.

"She gave a light nod with her head.

"'He calls me his darling and puts his arms around my body. He even kissed me once already.'

"I became angry and stomped my foot.

"'Just don't hit me,' she cried. 'He promises me beautiful clothes, expensive stones, and I often don't have enough to buy myself a ribbon; I could ride in his coach with four horses, but I don't want to.'

"She still didn't dare look up.

"'Look at me,' I said.

"She obeyed, but her eyes were so shy, so estranged.

"'I don't listen when he talks to me,' she continued eagerly, 'and I threaten to slap him when he kisses me.'

"'And yet he kissed you anyway,' I said, 'and you didn't slap him.'

"'I don't want him,' she cried again. 'He knows that and takes his revenge because of it. My father can no longer do anything right in his eyes. He'll end up taking his land away from him and chase us out of the village like beggars or thieves.'

"'He can't do that,' I told the silly thing. 'Just keep up your courage,' I said. 'If God blesses us, the devil can wait on us. Don't be afraid, my little soul, my sweet, my little quail. Do you still love me?—Hold on and stay firm.'

"'And then she began to cry, so miserably that it could make your heart burst.

"'I won't be able to!' she cried.

"Just then, a lark flew up out of the green field.

"'There's a lark flying,' she said, 'flying into heaven! Oh, if only I could go, too.'

"'Please, don't talk such nonsense,' I cried. 'Stay with me.'

"'It won't work,' she replied and sighed and wiped the tears out of her eyes. 'I won't be able to resist.'

"My horse tugged at me as if it wanted to say something. I stroked it sadly, and tears came to my eyes.

"'And why should you, anyway?' I said. 'No one can do anything that is against his nature.'

"In the meantime, Katharina had been carefully observing her reflection in the water. Oh, how beautiful she was! In the softly rocking mirror, her face was like that of a russalka, the water-nymph that no human soul can resist.

"'Will you remain faithful to me?' I asked her softly.

"A terrible anxiety gripped me. I was afraid of losing her, of being separated from her. I could have fallen on my knees and pleaded with her to stay with me! But—God forgive her.

"'I won't leave you!' she cried and threw herself into my arms. 'Oh, if I were as beautiful as the bright dawn, I would shine over all the fields and never fade—but now, I don't know what it is about me that he likes, and we fit together better, you and I. Isn't that so, Balaban?'

"I nodded and walked a little distance away with the horses without saying a thing."

The capitulant fell silent. His pipe had gone out while he was telling his story; he opened the lid, stuck his knife in so that the ashes flew out, and filled it up with fresh tobacco. Then he carefully placed a little piece of tinder on the flint that he carried on his belt and used his knife to strike fire. The sparks flew, and he placed the glowing tinder, which gave off a pleasant, bitter smell, in the pipe and took a few, shallow draughts.

"I talked to her again," he continued. "I went to her hut. The old man was doing his required labor for the estate owner, which we call robot, so we were alone. When I took her in my arms, she was trembling, and she kissed me until my lips bled. All at once, she smiled.

"'Just imagine what it would be like if I had a gentleman, a gracious, mighty lord here like I have you,' Katharina said to me. 'Would he sigh and roll his eyes like you do? Wouldn't that be something?'

"As she spoke, she leaned back and stared at the ceiling, her hands behind her neck, as if in a dream, I'm telling you. 'It's a proud pleasure,' she muttered, 'a man of such wealth and power! He whips the other women like dogs, but me—he kisses my hands. Don't you believe me?'

"Oh, I believed her, all right. She saw that I was close to tears, and that seemed to make her feel sorry. She slowly brushed the hair back from my forehead and smiled. When I said nothing for a long time, she stood up and combed her hair.

"'What's wrong with you!' she cried. 'Don't get me started, or—'

"Her eyes sparkled with anger.

"'Katharina,' I said, 'think of eternity!'

Kolanko shifted back and forth uneasily and looked sympathetically at the capitulant.

"'That's exactly what I'm thinking of,' she replied. 'We're here for a very short time, and we're there forever.'

"You didn't believe her, did you?" the old man interrupted him.

"She sat down next to me," the capitulant continued.

"'What would you say, Balaban,' she began, 'if I were to belong to the master here and then belong only to you on the other side? We'd be pure spirits there. And I'd be a pure spirit, too. I'm not one down here. Here I'm a woman like all the rest.'

"As she spoke, her eyes narrowed, you know, and her red mouth laughed so mischievously that a shiver ran down my spine.

"'If you had a farmstead,' she said, 'you could keep maids and hired hands for me, a coach and four horses. You could bring me expensive jewels and a sable from the city, like the ones the noblewomen wear. Oh yes, if you were even just a real farm-owner with a little money to his name, I'd love no one but you, you alone. In the whole world, you're the man who's dearest to me.'

"She put her arms around my neck and cried and kissed me. In my breast, sadness had made everything stand still. I thought and thought like a man lying in chains who's waiting to be hanged and doesn't know any way out.

"'You know what?' I finally said. 'I'll become a haydamak, a robber, so that you can have expensive jewels and gold and silver, sable furs and ermine.'

"'For what?' she asked, shaking her head. 'They'll take you prisoner in the end and hang you from the gallows, and I can get everything from the master without harming a hair on his head. That's better, don't you think?'

"'You're being extremely good,' I replied.

"'Of course,' she cried. 'I don't want you to die because of me.' And she put her arms around my neck and kissed me softly on my eyelids, which were wet with tears. Then her father came in, looked at us, and put his flail in the corner. Out of politeness, I stayed and talked with him for a while and then left the house. It was a mild evening. The sky was twinkling. Katharina was walking alongside me. We were both silent. Then I started to walk faster, and she was left behind. I whistled for all I was worth, but it didn't come from the heart.

"All of that occurred long before 1848, you know. We still were bound by the laws of servitude and mandatory labor for the estate owners, and the peasants had to put up with a lot from the masters.

"Around that time, I was sent off with a load of salt for a few days. That was in violation of the rights granted to us peasants by Kaiser Joseph II, and I knew it, but I put up with it, and that wasn't good. You see, that was my misfortune; that's when my misery began. You should not do anything out of weakness. A person like that who submits to anything in spite of his ideas, his feelings or his desires will become negligent in his duties and turn into a really dishonest person. Well, thank God, I turned myself around in time. A man must do his duty; that's all there is to it."

"Well, but what should you have done?" the cardboard man asked with a sullen twitching of his eye.

"That was a difficult time!" Kolanko cried and sighed pitifully. "If you talked about your rights, the nobleman answered with his cane. Bad times! Bad times! You young people don't know much about it."

"Well, and what happened when they sent you off with the load of salt?" I asked quickly, for I know that when our peasants start talking about the bad old days, they never finish.

"Well, I was gone for a long time.

"When I came back, the mandatar[4] always had a lot of work for me, and Katharina anxiously avoided me. I could smell the tobacco right away. Finally I met my beloved in the church; we ran into each other quite by accident. She was wearing a silk kerchief, coral beads covering her whole neck, and a new sheepskin that you could smell from twenty paces. She barely looked me in the eye, and she was as white as freshly laundered lace.

"'You are beautiful,' I told her. 'Where's my kerchief?'

"'Look for it yourself!' she cried, part angrily and part timidly.

"I looked at her.

"'Are you going to harm me?'

"'Oh, no!' I said. 'Get out of here.'

"Sometimes I was sent off to cut wood in the forest. I felt good there. When the wind rushed through the tree-tops and the grasses bowed down, the woodpecker solemnly hammered on the trunks, a vulture floated in the sky above me, occasionally beating his wings lightly and crying, then I would lie on my back, look up into the sky, and my heart no longer pained me. My spirits were often low. I dug a hole under the roots of an oak and put one groschen after another there; I wanted to save enough to buy a flintlock. It would have taken a long time.

"While cutting wood, I ran into Brigitta, an old baba[5] from Tulava who was gathering thyme. She clapped her hands together.

"'You're out here cutting wood, Balaban,' she cried, 'and in the meantime, the estate owner has gone and put your Katharina on a mattress.'

"'What are you saying!' I responded. 'Is she with him in his house?'

"'Of course! Lord Jesus, was that a story,' she went on. 'The housekeeper had to leave immediately; the master chased her off the property. This Katharina is in command now. When I bring mushrooms into the kitchen and she comes in, her whole head is covered with paper sausages, like a real lady, and she wears a floor-length dress and smokes a cigar like a great lord. I looked at her, but I didn't kiss her hand. Don't you know what you're supposed to do with my hand, she starts screaming right away. It belongs here, she says, and slaps me in the mouth. And slaps me again.'

"The old lady also told me that Katharina was living like the mistress of the house and that she was dressing like a queen, that she ate off silver plates, was riding a horse, and gave people a beating whenever her heart desired.

"'She's still nothing but the master's plaything,' I said.

"Back then, when I was alone in the forest, I used to think about becoming a robber, God forgive me the sin, a haydamak who would set fire to the nobles' estates and nail them by their hands and feet to the barn wall like birds of prey. My conscience, however, wouldn't stay quiet, and a voice spoke to me wherever I went: 'What do you want, peasant, son of a peasant? What do you think you're going to do with a gun? Do you think you can wage war all by yourself against the whole of humanity?'—I did finally calm down and stayed in the village, but I decided just to fulfill my obligations and to suffer no injury to my rights.

"Well. Then I ran into Kolanko, who was sliding around in the snow like a dog that's been shot at. My Katharina had had him beaten because he hadn't greeted her as respectfully as she demanded, and so he started talking to me and told me—"

"Just think," the old man eagerly interrupted him. "She was lording it over us like a real lady or even more. We know how a master like that used to keep his woman back then. The master had two teachers brought from the city for her; one of them was a Frenchman. She learned everything that a clerk learns or even a priest. Every week a package full of books would come to her in the mail. She read everything, even newspapers, whole bunches of them. There was a whole box made of fine wood filled with them in her room. And she learned how to play whole pieces of music; the people would stand under her windows in the evening and listen."

Mongol laughed knavishly and stirred the fire up with a piece of wood.

"People like that had better not think about God's justice," he murmured.

The old man coughed hard and a rumble like a cat's arose from deep in his chest.

The capitulant stared off into space with a gloomy eye. During the whole story, his face remained uninterested, rigid, morose, and disconsolate.

The boy looked over at the Mongol, unashamedly astonished.

"Why are you looking at me like that?" the latter asked distrustfully and withdrew his yellow face with its yellow, slit nose into its own deep wrinkles.

"How do you do that," the boy asked, "without letting it rain right into your nose?"

The whole group laughed. The Mongol, however, grabbed the boy by the ear, slowly pulled him towards himself, and then gently let him go.

"Did you feel sad about your former beloved?" I asked the former soldier. "Did it cause you a lot of pain back then?"

"I wouldn't say so," he answered, puffing on his pipe. I didn't think about revenging myself on her, either, but whenever I had anything to do with the master class, I'd get angry every time. I wanted to better myself, and I learned how to read and write and do math. I was, of course, too big to go to school, so I learned from the deacon, and I paid him with a chicken or a fat goose or black tobacco smuggled in from Hungary. And then I stuck my nose into everything I could find; I read the bible, the legends of the saints, the story of Czar Ivan the Terrible, the rights granted to us by the Empress Maria Theresia, Kaiser Joseph and Kaiser Franz, and I also read a lot of the laws and wrote up the peasants' complaints so they could take them to the district office. There was no one in the whole area, far or wide, who knew as well as I how to stir up the people against the nobility, these Polish lords. In the whole of Galicia there were probably not as many court cases as there were in our village, and I wrote them all up.

"When the district captain made a tour, people would already be standing along the road with complaints, and I had my hand in all of them. If I could cause trouble for the estate owner, I did. And when I did, my heart would laugh as cheerfully as a dove. They called me a troublemaker and made threats against me, but there was fear in the land and no one dared try anything against me."

"He'd beat up the splendid-looking Cossacks,"[6] Mongol shouted with a laugh. "He'd beat them up for no reason, in the tavern or on the street, wherever he found them. And he'd tell them it was because they were nothing but dogs."

"'But, don't you realize—' they'd protest.

"'Haven't you realized what you're doing? Do you come from the estate?'

"'But—'

"'Do you deny it?'

"'No.'

"'Well, then, you deserve it.'

"'Yes, but if everyone who deserved a beating got one, sir,' the Cossacks would cry, 'within a year, there'd be no hazel switches left in the whole empire—that's how many sticks you'd need, and where would you ever find enough benches?'"

The capitulant smiled.

"Finally, the mandatar summoned me," he continued, "and reproached me for provoking the peasants, for being a troublemaker and a rebel and a haydamak."

"'Throw him onto the bench,' he shouted so loudly that the blood caused his face to swell, and he retreated behind his people.

"'What good will that do us?' the Cossacks asked. 'He'll just kill one of us to pay us back.' And no one dared lay a hand on me.

"So the mandatar attacked me himself, snorting, his hair flying, his eyes completely white, and raised the rod in the air. I was able to catch hold of him, and I gently turned his hand around until it cracked like the bowl of a pipe when you twist it to let the tobacco juice out.

"I quietly took his rod and put it in the corner, all quite politely, of course; he was an authority figure, you know.

"From then on they left me completely in peace until, damn it, I ran into the 'mistress' on the street. Her coach was stuck in the mud, and her coachman was sitting on his bench and uselessly beating the horses to a pulp. When she saw me, she curled up in the corner like a cat and started trembling. I just watched.

"'Come help, boy,' the coachman shouted.

"So I helped. I lifted the little coach out of the mud and gave it a push to get it going, and then I grabbed the whip and let him have a few for having done such a bad job of driving the 'lady.'

"From that day on, she gave herself no rest, I know, until she had me conscripted."

"She was ashamed to have him around," Kolanko confirmed, "and so she sent him into the army."

"In those days, the estates gathered up the recruits," the capitulant reported. "The Cossacks dragged me into the courtyard where a wooden post was standing. They stripped me naked and measured me; the doctor tapped my chest and looked into my eyes without half paying attention. Then they registered me, and my fate was sealed. My mother went down on her knees to the mandatar, and the tears softly rolled down my father's face, and they were standing upstairs at the window and watching me stand there, miserable, like God created me, without pity. I was crying from rage. It didn't help. We didn't have any money. They made me swear the oath on the spot and put an imperial cap on my head. I was a soldier. When we marched off, everyone ran after us and cried, and the recruits cried too. Every one of them was wearing a little cross around his neck and carrying a little sack filled with earth that he had dug up from under the doorstep of his house. The drums were beating, the corporal ordered us to march, and we set off like dogs on a leash. We all sang a song together; oh, it was such a sad song. I marched along in silence, and when we'd gone some distance and the village and the forest and the church had sunk below the horizon and I couldn't see anything that was mine anymore, I thought about my situation and concluded: 'Good, you're serving the Kaiser. You know who you belong to.'

"And how did you like it as a soldier?" I asked with genuine interest.

"Well enough, sir," the capitulant replied, and the look in his eyes was wonderfully good-natured. "It was good. They demanded nothing of me that wasn't part of my duty, nothing more, nothing less, and I was glad to do it. I finally knew that I was a human being. First I went to Kolomea, learned the drill, first alone and then with others. When I finally learned to handle a gun, I felt proud and wished that there would be a war.

"And in the district capital, I saw that there was an order to the world. They treated us strictly, but fairly. There were no undeserved punishments and no unearned pay, and the people in the city looked at the soldiers with a kind of respect. And when I stood guard in front of the district office and listened to the peasants and how they talked with one another and found justice and help against the Polacks, I looked up at the emperor's eagle hanging over the door and thought: You're only a little bird, and you don't have any wings, but you're big enough to protect a whole people.

"Later, when we would be on parade and the yellow flag with the black eagle would flutter above our heads, I'd just look at it and be satisfied.

"In the regiment, we stuck together like people did in the village back home, all for one, one for all. We helped those who were in the right and punished any wrongdoers ourselves. At night, when the officers were sleeping in their quarters and the sergeants were sleeping with their wives, we'd quietly gather and hold court over the thieves, the swindlers, the dishonest card- and dice-players, and the drunkards who brought the company shame, and we accomplished more that the officers with their rod and iron.[7]

"And so a year passed, and one day we packed our sacks and marched off to Hungary. From Hungary to Bohemia, from Bohemia to Styria. As a soldier, you see a lot of countries as time goes on, and all of them belonged to our Kaiser, and you see different peoples, and your heart is humbled, and you see that conditions at home aren't the best. I saw more prosperity, more justice and humanity and more civilization[8] than back at home. I learned to respect the Germans and the Czechs, who speak a language like ours.

"I saw Saint Nepomuk lying in his silver coffin, and I also saw the cliff in which the king had had him locked up and the stone bridge with all those saints where they threw him into the water and where the five flaming stars floated above his head in the waves. In Styria, I saw people with two necks."

Against my will, I had to laugh about the former soldier's naive ethnography. He noticed it and fell silent.

"I remember how you came back the village the first time when you were on leave," Kolanko remarked with a certain satisfaction. "The white coat with the blue lapels[9] looked devilishly good on you. The women followed you with their eyes and whispered. My old lady said back then that Balaban was the best-looking man for ten miles around, and she knew what she was talking about, that's for certain. But he didn't want anything to do with women."

"The gentleman certainly knows," the capitulant turned towards me, "that our soldiers used to cry back then when they had to be discharged. They had left servitude, unpaid labor, despotism, and poverty behind and had gotten used to order, justice, and respect only to return to poverty and brute force. So when they called for people to be discharged, everyone in the company stood still. I was the only one—I don't know what I was thinking—to step forward. Everybody stared at me. Well, so then they sent me home.

"I came home, to my father's place. When I walked in with my gray soldier's coat and cap, he just stared at me and ran his trembling hand through his gray hair. I kissed his hand.

"'It's good that you're here,' he said.

"Then my mother came, and she screamed and laughed until the tears rolled down her face. I told them about the regiment and the countries where our garrison had been, and they gave me a report on the people in the village. The neighbors came, and we drank a lot of brandy.

"I didn't care what was going on. I walked around like a sick man. Nobody said a thing to me. And I was silent, too, but thought that the estate owner must have chased Katharina out of the house because everyone was so silent on the subject. The other thought I had was that she was still with him, but that he'd turn her out soon. That's what I was wishing for; I don't know why. What was I going to do with her after all that?

"I had often wanted to see her in need, shamed and miserable, and yet I would have helped her anyway.

"No one even mentioned her name, and I didn't dare ask. On Sunday, during high mass, I looked up into the choir for some reason. Who's sitting there? My Katharina, like a high-born lady. She was so beautiful, much more beautiful than in the time before I was called up, but so pale, so sick, so tired, and she had the big, dark circles for eyes that you see in the dying."

A strange, quiet light lay on the capitulant's calm face.

"My blood froze," he continued.

"'Who's that beautiful lady?' I asked a boy who didn't know me.

"He looked at me stupidly and said, 'That's the mistress, the estate owner's wife.'

"He had really married her, quite properly, at the altar; so the boy was right, and she was now mistress over me."

The capitulant smiled.

"I could have run into her every day," he said after a while. "But what good would that do? So I went to another village to work. Everything was finished anyway."

The capitulant was silent. His arms had fallen at his sides, and he was looking into the fire with his head bent forward. His bronzed features had again assumed their deep, serene earnestness, and his eyes again burned like large, calm fires. Everyone was silent. The land around us shimmered in a deep, sacred silence.

"Your story seems to be at an end," I said after a pause.

"Yes," the capitulant said with embarrassment.

"Well, there's really nothing special about your story," I said. "It happens all the time, and it happens to everybody. The thing that's special about your story is you yourself. Didn't you ever think about revenge or retribution?"

"No," he answered, staring quietly into the air in front of him. "For what? It was part of our nature. Am I supposed to take revenge for the fact that I'm a man and she's a woman?"

His answer surprised me and revived my most intense interest.

"So you never were vindicated," I said.

"Yes I was," he replied after some thought. "It was in 1846,[10] when I was on leave, and the country was suffering the misery brought on by the Polish revolution.

"It was in the last days of that upheaval, in February, a terribly severe winter. That night, an especially deep snow had fallen and drifted over all the streets and paths. Wait a minute. That comes later. Everything's going around in my head in such a strange way right now. I have to tell you about something else first. It was like this. A certain unrest had been noticeable for some time; the estate owners were running back and forth in their coaches, and there were rumors about hidden weapons.

"There were quite a few peasants gathered in the tavern of Tulava, among them the judge, when our estate owner came and said to the peasants: 'Are you going to stick together with us nobles, or whose side are you going to be on? If you stick together with us, come to the church tonight, and I'll give you guns and go with you.'

"The judge responded to him: 'We're not going to stick together with you. We'll side with God and the Kaiser.' So the estate owner withdrew, and the judge spoke to the people: 'I don't want any of you people siding with these slave drivers and going off to help them.'

"Our estate owner, the same one who had made my Katharina his woman, left a document behind in the tavern. Everybody looked at it, but nobody could read. So the judge said: 'Go get Balaban. As an old soldier, so to speak, he'll know what to do with it.' So they called me, and I read the document for them.

"Up top it said: 'To all Poles who can read.'[11]

"I had to laugh out loud, because first there were no Poles there, and second, nobody who could read but me. So there it said—you must remember the nonsense from back then—there it said: 'Servitude and enforced labor arose through violence and injustice, for in earlier times all men were equal, and the nobles, farmers like us, usurped the authority over us and in the end sold the country to the Muscovites, the Prussians, and the Kaiser, whose German officials join the nobles in taking advantage of the peasants to such an extent that they can barely still their hunger and clothe themselves in miserable canvas. The Kaiser doesn't know anything about the peasants; he sells salt and tobacco to them at high prices so that he can live well in Vienna. Help can only come from God, but in order to attain that, everyone in the whole country has to rise up and take up weapons. The nobles recognize the injustices they've committed and wish to unite with the country people against the Kaiser and chase the German officials out of the country.'

"There was some truth in the document, and we thought it was good, but, we said to each other, that's not the way it is. It was nothing but a joke. Who used force against us if not the nobility? And who protected us against them as well as they could but the German officials and our Kaiser? No one wanted anything to do with the Poles.

"'If you follow the nobility,' I said, 'won't they work the peasants like you do the oxen now? Let's assemble in the tavern tonight just in case.'

"And so the night approached.

"As I said before, it was a hard winter, kind of like this one, and that night even more snow than usual had fallen. Everything was drifted over. You couldn't see a single road or footpath. Only the forests loomed like black walls in the bright, white night.

"We had gathered in the tavern, and everybody had brought his flail or his scythe with him. I took a group of peasants, it was around midnight, and formed a patrol. The peasants were pretty afraid and were expecting a bad end to the matter. I talked some courage into them and said: 'If we are brave and resist them, we have nothing to fear from the rebels.'

By that time a few sleighs with nobles and leaseholders and other parasites were on there way to the estate. When they caught sight of us, they stopped, and one of them stood up and shouted that we should join them, that the revolution had broken out, the peasants were free and we were welcome to break open the imperial safes and attack the Jews.

"'There are no traitors here,' I shouted. 'We're on the side of God and the Kaiser.'

"I hadn't even finished when the Poles began firing. I took some hits from their shot, and one of the peasants got a bullet in the foot. I screamed at the peasants: 'Forward!' So we attacked the Poles from the left and the right, tore them out of their sleighs, and took them all prisoner. I hit one of them over the head because he wouldn't give up, but the rest of them were unhurt. Then shooting broke out near the tavern, and I ran as fast as I could, but when I got there, it was all over. Bobroski, one of the nobles, was lying in his own blood in the snow, and our estate owner was standing in the middle of a bunch of peasants, and they were beating him from all sides. They would have beaten him to death if I hadn't shown up; the blood was already running down his head. I saved him.

"You?"

"Me, sir. I was sorry, I have to admit that the peasants didn't beat him to death, but once I got there I couldn't let it happen. The Poles would have said that it was out of revenge for Katharina, and that would have left a nasty stain on our cause.

"We tied his hands and his feet, like we did with all the others, threw them all onto their own sleighs, and drove the whole pack of rotten nobles to the district office in Kolomea where I delivered about twenty nobles, their money, watches, and rings, everything, which was the proper thing to do. Oh, they were good times, sir! A poor man's war against his oppressor, and order maintained everywhere as if it were a commandment; our lookouts were at all the intersections, and peasants in ragged canvas coats walked into the district office and pulled money by the thousands out of their pockets and faithfully laid it on the table. We let them shoot at us, and then we disarmed them, and everyone would have sacrificed his own blood. Everyone thought that all differences would have to end now, that every man would be as free as any other. Everyone equal, everyone! Then in the west, the Polish peasants began to murder and a large number of military were marched into the country. Everything turned out differently than we expected. But two years later, serfdom was abolished, and the peasant is now a free man."

"What happened to your estate owner?" I asked.

"He was taken to the fortress in chains," Kolanko cried. "His little wife consoled herself with one of the neighbors until he was freed again in '48[12] with all the other Polish rebels."

"That's when I re-enlisted," Balaban said, "and returned to the regiment. We marched off to the Hungarian war, crossing the Carpathians in the winter, and there were a lot of battles. Then we had to come back, and we were hit by a bad winter; people were left lying on the road, smiling, and they fell asleep and froze.

Finally we chased the Magyars until Kossuth fled Hungary like a squirrel running out of a forest.

"Strange times, sir! People died, one after the other, one felled by a bullet, another by a saber, some drowned or died along the road after they pulled out their little sack with the earth from their village, and every one of them would have preferred to go on living. Only I didn't die, and everything passed me by. It made me have my doubts about everything. Where was the justice in that? Then I was discharged and came home, since my father was dead."

"It wasn't because of her?"

"For what?" Balaban replied with a shrug of his shoulders. "I'm a former soldier and she's a lady! So I came back. My father was dead. My mother too. I was alone. The land was free, but everything else had been sold off except for the shack and a few fruit trees. So how would you like that? There was an awful lot to be done."

"I'd always had a liking for animals and breeding, and so I started studying the bees and their behaviors and set up a lovely bee garden, near the house. You know it, don't you? Then I raised two big dogs, real wolves—their father really was a wolf; I'd seen him. They were beautiful dogs, gray with eyes that shone like torches at night; well, you've seen them. I took over the post of watchman for the village fields. I had a tomcat, too," the capitulant smiled, just like every Galician peasant does when he talks about cats. "I pulled him out of the water."

"You should see the dogs, sir," the cardboard man remarked with a quiet, but envious admiration.

"Well, he's earned them," Kolanko cried. "We've never had someone to protect the fields as well as he does. The village should thank God."

"Oh, come on," the capitulant said dismissively. "Don't make the gentleman uncomfortable with that kind of talk."

"No, it's really a pleasure to hear about anything concerning you," I replied.

"You're too kind."

"This is a man, for a change, who does his duty," the cardboard man said seriously, pointing at Balaban. "I don't like praising anyone, but it's the truth. The thieves are afraid of him and the drunks turn sober when they see him at night. When he collects the taxes, we get more than when we've sent twenty men."

"At election time, the peasants listen to him more than to the judge," the Mongol asserted. "If you want to be elected from this district, sir, just tell the capitulant. He can do anything with our people that he wants."

"Please stop, neighbors," the capitulant repeated, quite modestly. "What else does a man have but his duty?"

"Nothing, is what I say," Kolanko squealed. "When you start talking about women—oho!—he's quite a moralist. We have a girl in the village. She's got red hair and is as pretty as a star in the heavens. You'd think she was a countess, to look at her. But she's a frivolous thing. One night he ran into her when she was sneaking out of the village.

"'Running after somebody again?' my Balaban barked at her. 'What good does it do you? It's so easy for something unfortunate to happen, and then he'll leave you. You'd be better off taking a husband.'

"'But she just laughs and says she won't take just anybody who comes along, but if he wanted to marry her, he could have her on the spot."

"What did he say?"

"He just shook his head and kept on preaching."

"He doesn't want to take a wife," said Mrak, who had been listening carefully and was now continuing his watch.

"Oh! He still loves the other one," suddenly cried the Jew, who had woken up and approached our circle. His dumb, cunning face was disfigured by a repulsive laugh.

"Listen," said the capitulant. "Your head is like a steam bath, and your tongue sweats and doesn't understand what's dripping off it."

We all had a good laugh. My Jew looked especially at me with a hurt air, pulled down the sleeves of his coat, brushed off his knees with the palm of his hand, and uncharacteristically stormed back to his horses, grabbed their reins, and yanked their heads back and forth with the result that they looked at him sympathetically.

"Is that so?" Kolanko asked the capitulant in all seriousness, taking him gently by the elbow.

"Is it true that you can't forget her?" the cardboard man asked hesitatingly.

The capitulant remained silent.

He calmly turned his gentle, honest, sad face towards us. His eyes had again taken on a damp look, filled with understanding, that was painful just to see. I felt so strange at that moment. Nature's deep silence was reproduced in my soul, and just as the lonely fire calmly sent its smoke upwards, a melancholy memory slowly arose in front of me. And a wonderfully beautiful pale face framed by dark, bacchantic curls arose from the ashes with half closed, tenderly shy eyes.

"What stupidity! What a piece of stupidity!" the Mongol shouted, and everything sank away, and the shadow that remained was devoured by the fire's greedy tongues.

"You should spit at the ground under the feet of the pretty mistress of Zavala," the cardboard man screamed.

"That such a man should love such a beast," Kolanko joined in.

"Don't get yourselves so worked up," the capitulant said coldly. He had become visibly pale, and his eyebrows and his eyebrows had narrowed darkly. "You see, it was quite natural. The poor girl had led a miserable life and then had the opportunity to become the mistress of the estate. The estate owner was a handsome man, wasn't he? I was good enough as long as nobody better was there. After all, would I serve some petty lord if I could serve the Kaiser? You can't try to understand that with your heart. Between a man and a woman, the heart is the least important thing. Let's look at it rationally.

"Do you love with your heart, comrade, when you want to have a woman in bed? Do you only want her to love you or do you want her to be yours? Do you like it better for her unwillingly to be your wife or for her heart to belong to you while she belongs to another? I've thought about all of that. I've had enough time for it. These days, people are always talking about what humans have in common with animals, aren't they?

"Well, I'm telling you, relationships between men and women are about nothing but the struggle to survive, like everywhere else. Do you understand?"

"No."

I had begun to understand where his thoughts were heading and was amazed. His ideas were flowing, his eyes glowing, and he was speaking really well, with the natural eloquence of our people.

"You see, the only thing I learned as a soldier was to be contemptuous of death. It would even be better to learn to wish for it, to love it. All unhappiness comes from our love for life, and that includes our unhappiness with women. As miserable as this life is, everyone does everything he can in order to go on living. If I say a single word that isn't true, shoot me. Well, then. A woman lives on love, on the love of a man. Do you understand?"

Kolanko nodded vigorously. Everyone was listening with the utmost attention; even the dog raised its foxlike head toward the capitulant.

"I think you're right," I said. "Everything bows to necessity. Every living thing feels how sad existence is, and yet they all struggle desperately to cling to it. Humans struggle with nature and with other humans, and men struggle with women, and their love is nothing but another example of the struggle for existence. Both want to go on living in their children. Everyone wants to see his face, his eye, and his soul live again in their children, and everyone wants to become a better, more perfect being by appropriating to himself the superior qualities of the other.

"In addition, woman, both for their own sakes and for the sake of their children, want to use their men in order to live. I don't know if I've expressed myself very well."

"Perfectly," the whole circle shouted encouragingly.

"If the gentleman will allow," the capitulant continued, "I'll say what I think of that, in my own way as I understand it."

"Let me talk," the old man shouted, threateningly lifting his pillow. "You do all the talking. Let me talk first."

"Go ahead."

"Now, what was it I wanted to say?"

"Now he doesn't know what he wants to say."

"Well—" the old man got stuck again.

We laughed.

"Go ahead and laugh. I know what it was," he said blithely. "This is the way it is. A woman has to eke out an existence just like a man, but how should she do it? She has to put up with some things that a man doesn't. How is she supposed to work when she has a child? Or when she has to spend her time bringing it up? And she might have another one every year. She can't work like a man does. Nature hasn't given her any stamina, and she hasn't learned anything worthwhile, no trade or anything, so of course she tries to live off a man or uses him to make her fortune. Look at all a man has to do to climb up in the world, while a pretty young thing just has to show her face, or sometimes a little more, and suddenly she's changed from a milkmaid to a grand lady. Am I right or not?"

"You're right, old man!"

"So if you'll let me continue," the capitulant began speaking again. "I've stopped struggling and sinning like the others. I was defeated once, and that was enough.

"It's better if I can say to myself that my eye will someday be extinguished and my soul at rest. I think men are better off without women. It's not the woman who goes looking for the man; it's the other way around. That's where the advantage lies for her, and she can base her calculations on the man's interest. What else should a woman want but to gain some advantage out of the man's miserably ridiculous situation?

"If you find someone standing in the water up to his neck, stuck in the mud and ready to drown, and he has a bag of money, and you can save him, he'll be glad to throw it onto the shore for you.

"But a smart woman isn't satisfied with a bag of money. She drags the man off to a priest.

"Do you understand me? That's why there is such a great enmity among women, just like there is among tailors or basket-weavers. Every one of them is trying to sell her little basket as best she can. And is she wrong to do so?

"Isn't the woman judged by who her husband is? Once a girl from the village marries a count, she's a countess, isn't she? Her husband's honored position is hers, and that's why a woman is always prouder of his titles and his wealth than the man is himself. You understand?"

"I still don't understand," Mrak replied angrily, "how you can love the Lady of Zavala, your sweet Katharina, who betrayed you so miserably."

"You'll never understand it," the capitulant said drily.

"And no woman is worth what a man will suffer for her," I said softly.

"Indeed, sir," the capitulant answered. "No woman is worth what a man feels for her, except for his mother. But as to the mistress, what did she actually do to me? I wasn't born under a lucky star. And besides, I've lived long enough to see this one and that one fall in love and kiss and marry happily, only to have his wife start lifting her skirts to hurt him. If she had become my wife, I might have started beating her before much time had gone by. None of it matters, this way or that; it's all the same.

"A man's love soon comes to an end, and I say that women are right to look to their interests while they can, as long as they're young and pretty, and as long as the man's head is on fire; a fire like that is soon extinguished, and a little woman soon becomes old."

I shook my head.

"What's bothering you, sir?"

"That you talk only about this natural love while you yourself bear witness to another kind of love."

"I haven't said anything against that," the capitulant replied heatedly. "Of all people, I'm the least likely to pretend it doesn't exist. A man can love with his heart if it pleases him, why not? But a woman can't do that. I'm telling you, a woman might want to give a man the same kind of feelings back that he feels for her—she might want to, but it's not possible.

"How my horse looks at me when I show it my love, so human almost, and it seems as if it wants to talk to me, but it can do nothing more than snuggle up to me. And it seems sad because of that, but the next morning it's just as happy to carry somebody else on its back. Should I make accusations against the two of them because of that? And to who?"

Kolanko smiled craftily with his tightly closed lips. "The Jew knows why he prays every day," he said. "Thank you, Lord, for not making me a woman."

"If you're in love, with real emotion," the capitulant continued, "you'd better yield to your fate and renounce it in time; otherwise, you'll be led around by the nose in the most amusing way, for a woman in love is like a Jew making a deal."

"What are you saying about the Jews?" my coachman grumbled.

"In the end," the capitulant said quietly, "our entire wisdom consists of the words: renounce, suffer, and stay silent.

"And if you're surprised that I've kept my feelings for Katharina for so long, why do you think that an honest love has to possess its object no matter what the cost? You don't love someone because they are good or bad or moral, for example. Oh, no! And I don't love her because she acted fairly toward me or not. You only love someone when you have to, when nature leaves you no choice, so to speak, and forcibly attaches you to one person. And that's the only kind of love that will suffer whatever comes with it, mockery, ridicule, beatings, abuse, or cruelty, and that kind of love doesn't even ask if it's requited. And not even time, which kills everything else, can kill it."

"You would have made an excellent husband," the old man said after a pause. "Why don't you take a wife? Anyone would happily give you his daughter and add a house and land and some money as well."

"It's impolite to refuse," the capitulant replied, "but have I asked that favor of any of you? How should I take a wife? This is the first time that I've talked to you about this. You know me now. I've loved so honestly with my whole heart. How can I love another woman, and if that kind of love is missing, why should I marry? Am I an animal?"

"You're right, when you look at the matter carefully," Kolanko added, "especially since everything fades with the passage of time."

"Not everything," the capitulant with his beautiful, illuminating gaze.

"And yet," he sighed a little later, "what you've said is true. Even our senses weaken more and more. Eventually, things that caused us pain come to be almost a pleasure. You think of feelings that have died like you think of people that have died. What do you say about that, comrade?

"It's so sad when you finally know that what you feel doesn't last. My heart ached when I buried my parents, and now I sometimes dream, for example, that I'm drinking brandy with my father, and he's quite drunk. How do you like that?

"Or I know that when something exists today, it might not exist in a year. Everything passes like the clouds that drift away at evening time, even bad things.

"The human will can do anything. Disease and death are the only things it can't conquer.

"When the sergeant would cross a week off the calendar every Saturday, showing no feeling at all, I'd be so sad, but that's nothing. Sadder than the passage of time and of life is the change that we note in ourselves, in our thoughts and our feelings. That is what dying really is. Isn't it natural? You see something new every day, everything changes around you. It's one thing when you're a child and another when you're a man. So can you remain the same person? And can you demand of others that they not change?"

Everyone was quiet for a moment, and then we heard the soft tinkling of a bell, far, far away, and endlessly pitiful.

"That's somebody dying," the old man said and blessed himself.

"What are you talking about?" Mrak replied. "It's the nobles returning from their conspiracies in Tulava. Listen!"

The capitulant rose, carefully extinguished his pipe, and stuck it in his boot. Then he slowly walked out into the night, stopped, took his cap off, inhaled through his mouth and his nose, and held out the palms of his hands.

The little bell came closer and closer.

The capitulant put his cap back on.

"The cold is letting up. The wind has changed directions."

He then returned to the fire and picked up his flintlock.

"All right, people, get ready to carry out your duty."

They all got up immediately and surrounded the capitulant with their scythes and flails.

"A sleigh! Get ready!" Mrak shouted from the grove of trees.

The desperate little bell was already quite nearby, and we could hear the coachman's whip crack like a pistol shot as well as the snorting of the horses.

Then the peasant patrol ordered the sleigh to stop.

"Stop! Stop!" they all cried and ran over to the sleigh.

There the sleigh stood in front of us, and out of the bearskins that covered it there arose a beautiful, slender woman in a luxurious fur. When she pulled back her veil, she was even more beautiful, but terribly pale. Her blue eyes were feverish with anger.

"What do you want?" she shouted with a voice that was choked with anger.

"Your passport," the watch replied laconically.

"I don't have one."

"Authorizations?"

"I have none."

"Then you are under arrest," Mrak cried and grabbed the horses' reins.

Then the capitulant stepped forward, his flintlock on his shoulder, and pulled Mrak off to the side.

The others quickly joined them.

"Let her go," the capitulant said in a half-whisper.

"Let her go—without a pass—why?"

"I know her," he replied. "Let her go."

"You do know her, don't you," the old man said seriously. "Let her go."

The capitulant had returned to the fire and was stoking its flames.

The others slowly followed suit.

"Go on and leave," the patrol said ironically.

The woman sank back into her fur, the coachman cracked his whip, and the sleigh flew off on its snowy way.

The Jew laughed.

"Who was it?" I asked in an aside.

"Her."

"Her?"

The cardboard man nodded and then poked around in the fire.

"That was the mistress of Zavala," the old man whispered. "The one that he loved and that he still loves."

We were silent for a long time.

Then the cardboard man said, "They say she isn't happy with her husband either. She's always got tailors from the court down there, and did you see how pale she was?"

"Oh, but did you see the sleigh and the horses?" cried the capitulant. "And her Cossacks? The great lords kiss her hand—and the beautiful fur that she has. Why shouldn't she be happy?"

NOTES

1. A soldier who voluntarily undergoes a second or third period of military service—called a "capitulation" in Austria.

2. The messengers of the Polish emigration.

3. The long, hooded outer coat of our peasants; made of unshorn, shaggy cloth.

4. Representative of the nobleman in management and legal issues.

5. Derisive name for an old woman; also the name of an Easter cake.

6. In the Poland of old, every great noble had his own soldiers, usually Cossacks, and even today, some of the servants in every estate house are dressed in the Cossack uniform.

7. The Galician soldier applies the self-government of his community, as well as the popular court (lynch justice), to his regiment and his company.

8. The word is known to the Galician peasants and was used in striking fashion by the peasant deputies in the provincial parliament of 1861, as was the word "humanity."

9. The uniform of the Parma infantry regiment, which has Kolomea as its recruiting area.

10. 1846 was the year of the Polish revolution and the counter-revolution of the Galician peasants.

11. Title of a manifesto of the Polish revolutionary government.

12. The general amnesty after the March revolution in Vienna.

Moonlight

It was a clear, warm August night. I was coming down from the mountain, my rifle over my shoulder, and my big, black English labrador was tiredly following me, step by step, with his tongue hanging out. We had lost our way. More than once I stood still, looked around, and tried to figure out which way to go. Every time I did, my dog sat down and looked at me.

Before us lay a gently forested series of hills. The full red moon stood over the blue-black trees and cast a dazzling light upon the dark skies. The white stream of stars flowed grand and calm from east to west, and the Great Bear was standing low on the northern horizon. Between the nearby trunks of the willows a light transparent haze arose from a small swamp that was quivering with a dull green shimmer. The groanlike cry of a bittern could be heard in the reeds. As we proceeded, the landscape was more and more filled with light. On both sides, the gloomy tree trunks slowly receded, and before us appeared the gently waving plain, a green, shimmering sea upon which a white estate house with its large poplars swam like a ship under full sail. From time to time, a soft stream of air drifted through the grasses and leaves, and with it came a wondrous sound. As I came nearer, it unfolded its melancholy beauty. It was a good piano, and a fine and practiced hand was playing Beethoven's *Moonlight Sonata*. It seemed to me as if a wounded human soul were casting its tears onto the keys. A despairing dissonance—then the instrument fell silent. I was barely a hundred paces from the courtyard of the small, isolated estate with its bleakly rustling, dark poplars. A dog sadly rattled its chain, and a distant stream sang monotonously and plangently into the night.

A woman appeared at the top of the steps at the entrance to the house, rested with both arms on the banister, and gazed down at the ground. She was tall and slender. Her pale face glowed in the moonlight like phosphorous, her dark hair wound into a voluptuous crown and flowing down over her white shoulders. She heard my footsteps, stood up, and when I stopped at the foot of the stairs, she fixed her big, dark, moist eyes on me. I explained my story and asked for shelter for the night.

"Everything that is ours," she said with a deep, soft voice, "is at your service. We so rarely have the pleasure of receiving a guest. Follow me."

I climbed the rotting wooden steps, took the small, trembling hand that the mistress of the house had extended to me, and followed her through the open door into the house.

We entered a large, square room with whitewashed walls, the entire furnishings of which consisted of an old gaming table and five wooden chairs. The gaming table was missing a leg, and one of the problematic chairs had been shoved under it with a pile of bricks on its seat to support the shaky table-top. Four men were sitting at the table playing tarot. The owner of the estate, a little man with blunt, firm features, deep-set, little blue eyes, a short dry mustache, and shortly cropped blond hair stood up to greet me, holding his pipe firmly with his teeth while offering me his hand. While I repeated my tale and my request, he organized his cards and nodded his head to indicate agreement. Then he sat down on his chair again and took no further notice of me.

The lady had a chair brought in from the adjoining room and placed at the corner of the table. Then she left us to make the necessary arrangements, leaving me time to observe the group.

First there was the Russian priest from the neighboring village, with an athletic frame and muscles, the neck of a bull, and a stupid, alcoholic face which years of schnaps had burned into all possible shades of red. He smiled incessantly and sympathetically, occasionally taking tobacco from a tall, oval, wooden container, stuffing it into his flat, upturned nose, and finally taking a blue handkerchief with fantastic Turkish flowers from his breast pocket and wiping his mouth. Next to him sat one of our host's neighbors, a relaxed lease-holder in a black, laced-up jacket who sang through his nose untiringly and smoked the strongest, blackened cigars. The third was a cavalry officer with thinning hair and an immobile black mustache. He had been billeted in the house and had made himself comfortable. He was without a tie, in an open summer jacket with worn cuffs. His face was immobile when he played, but he steamed when he lost and drummed on the table with the fingers of his right hand. They invited me to join them in a game, but I excused myself by saying I was tired. We soon were given a cold dinner and some wine.

The mistress of the house returned, sat down in a small brown armchair that the cossack rolled in, and lit a cigarette. She took a sip from my glass and handed it to me with a charming smile. We chatted about the sonata she had played with so much understanding, about Turgenev's first book, about the Russian acting troupe that had given a few performances in Kolomea, about the harvest, the communal elections, the peasants, who had begun to drink coffee, and about the fact that the number of plows in the village had increased since the abolition of serfdom. She laughed out loud and rolled around in her chair. The moon was shining directly on her.

Suddenly she fell silent, closed her eyes, complained, after a while, about a headache, and went to her room. I whistled for my dog and retired as well.

The cossack led me through the courtyard. Suddenly he stood still and looked up at the moon with a foolish smile. "What power that has over men and animals," he said. "Betyar, our dog, howls at it all night long, and the cat sings on the rooftop, and when it shines into our cook's face, she talks in her sleep and predicts the future. I swear on my mother's love that it's all true."

My room look out the back toward the garden, from which a narrow terrace led up to my window. I opened it and leaned out.

From its lofty height, the full moon was pouring its solemn and sacred light over the landscape; it floated purely and cloudlessly above me, and the enigmatic world of its surface lay upon its disk like a faint aroma, like the delicate tracery on a crystal lamp illuminated from within. Not a single cloud could be seen against the deep blue heavens; there was not even a light, glowing haze, interwoven with moonlight, to conceal it with mysterious veils. Only the stars flared up now and again like sparks being extinguished. Endless and dreamily silent, the plains of my homeland stretched off to the east. Big, milky white ears of corn leaned over the garden fence toward me and in the distance, fields alternated with fields like on a monstrous chess board, white rye alternating with brown buckwheat and dark pasture land. Here and there, black sheaves of corn huddled together like peasants' huts. A lonely fire was burning on the horizon and slowly and silently sending its silvery gray smoke heavenwards. Shadows floated across it and disappeared and from somewhere nearer me, muffled bells rang out from time to time, and horses, grazing with their front legs fettered, made an occasional, strange appearance. And from where you could hear the scythes ring out sharp and bright, mighty haystacks glowed in a damp mist; the meadow lay in a wet shimmer; gaunt, black well pumps stretched toward the sky; and dark molehills stood like distant fortifications. And the rapid, flashing mountain stream cut the land in two, bordered by swamps as if by pieces of a shattered mirror.

A white cat prowled noislessly through the garden on velvet paws, shimmering like snow between the high grass, which moved softly and now and then gave off a sad, yearning sound like the cooing of a dove or the obstinate sobbing of a sleepy child. The cat jumped over the fence and a short while later appeared off to the left, at the foot of a dam that ran from the estate to the village like the ruin of a Tartar wall. She soundlessly climbed up on it and sat softly whimpering at the edge of the pond, seemingly observing herself in its dull, silver mirror. Big-leaved water lilies spun a green cover upon the water like a piece of lace regularly pierced by white and yellow flowers, which flared up in the blue moonlight like colorful flames.

The lovelorn little sleepwalker stretched her smooth limbs and walked softly past the high, luminescent reeds, past the pale water lilies, the rowboat groaning at its chain, and the sleeping swan towards the deep, steaming forest which, illuminated by the moon, stood in the distance like a smooth, polished wall. All around in the damply glistening bushes, the nightingales sang, and one of them began sobbing quite near, in the garden, so sweetly and heartbreakingly. The heavy fruit trees filtered the clear light of the moon with their countless black leaves, and yet every blade of grass glowed and every flower glittered with a magic fire. Every time that the air wafted softly through the garden, a liquid silver trickled over the lawn, the gravel paths, and the raspberry canes under my window. The red poppies began to burn; the melons lay like golden spheres in the green beds; the water barrel seemed to be filled with silver; the lilacs, covered with glowworms, stood in the damp haze like Moses' burning bush, and lightning bugs flew upwards from them like sparks. The honeysuckle arbor, filled with moonlight and illuminated from within, arose from the garden like a chapel in which an eternal lamp was burning. The aroma of lilac and thyme welled up, and an occasional breath of air carried the smell of the meadows' fresh hay into the garden.

The whole of nature was slumbering softly in the chaste light of the full moon and seemed to be struggling to express itself. The water sang its one note uninterruptedly; the air rustled the leaves on the trees from time to time; the nightingales sobbed; the grasshoppers whirred; here and there, a tree-frog croaked; in the windowsill on which I was leaning, a woodworm was busily tapping away; and above my head, swallows were twittering in their consecrated nest. And then the moonlight night began to resound, and the light, the aroma, and the melodies became one: the mistress of the house was playing the *Moonlight Sonata*. I felt wondrously calm, and when she had finished, the trees and the nightingales fell silent; only the woodworm continued its tapping.

A severe motionlessness and a deep silence filled the entire countryside until a sharp, fresh wind rose and carried the harmonious snatches of a melancholy folk-song to my ear.

It was the reapers, who were using the cool, bright night and working hard. In the moonlight. I clearly saw them moving around the yellow fields like ants.

Everything was silent. Only man was awake in his misery, laboring in the sweat of his brow for the sake of this absurd existence that he passionately loves and despises in equal measure. From the dawning morning until late at night, all his thoughts are directed with blind obstinacy towards its maintenance; his heart constricts as if in a cramp, and his poor head becomes feverish when he sees it threatened or believes that what he considers to be its enjoyments or its dignity is being cut short or stolen; and even in sleep, his brain continues working toward tomorrow and the day after and on and on, and in his dreams, life's images torment him. Innate in him is a perpetual agitation that seeks to secure and protect his attainments; he builds and acquires for eternity, whether he plows the loose earth that provides the eternally cooking hearth of his existence or steers his little vessel through the world's oceans, whether he observes the course of the stars or chronicles the fates and the history of his clan with childish industry—he studies, thinks, designs, and invents with the sole purpose of keeping his sad machinery running, and he would sacrifice his best ideas at any time for a piece of bread. Life is what he wants, life above all else, life and nourishment for his little lamp that threatens at every moment to be extinguished forever.

And that is the reason for his anxious need to reproduce his life in new creatures to whom he leaves behind the testament of his joys, but who inherit nothing but his pains, his struggles, and his suffering. How he loves them, his heirs, how he protects them and cares for them and raises them as if they were his own beloved self multiplied by three or even ten!

And as inventive as he is in propagating his own existence and in exploiting it in his own way, he shows himself to be just as untiring and ruthless in endangering, threatening, and plundering the existence of others for his own benefit. He cheats, he steals, he robs, and he murders without respite. He sets up mad, complicated theories in order to helplessly subjugate whole races of his fellow beings. Without a single thought he has condemned and branded animals and men of different color or different language, and he has done so only in order to live at the expense of the living.

It is an eternal and bloody war, one day waged quietly from hearth to hearth and forge to forge, the next day fought loudly and noisily on battlefields and oceans, and always under holy but fraudulent flags, and always without mercy and without end.

And yet, there is renunciation, austere and blessed, in whose assured peace lies the only happiness that is granted us, peace, quiet, sleep, and death. And why do we all tremble so in the face of death, who releases us from all doubt and who stills all pain! Why does the lamp in our breast flicker so anxiously when the icy breath of destruction touches us? How we cling to our memories, how strongly we desire only to live on within our own selves! To remember no more, to think no more, to dream no more—the creature is gripped with such fear and such despair, and it is overcome with a deep, incurable horror in soundless nights.

Incurable? No. Curable indeed, but only with the aid of thought. Its light gives us support everywhere; cold and bright, but not unfriendly, it shines into the dark and the abyss, and it gradually illuminates our soul, disperses the shadows that frighten us, and makes us humble, calm, and serene.

And as the still, soft light of the moon shines into my soul, familiar, dear figures rise transfigured before me, and like exiled gods, the hallowed ideals of forgotten times file past like big, white, quiet clouds; people whom I'd loved and were now separated from me by coldness or hatred or who had long been covered by the earth; the sublime images of perfection from a golden, resolute youth—He who spoke to His people among thunder and lightning on Mount Sinai and that greater one who, the crown of thorns upon his head, loaded the cross of humanity onto His bloody, flayed back. Dismembered snatches of fog drift in the moonlight like precious, tattered old flags and wilted flowers and withered wreaths. And a beloved woman, with luxurious blond braids and a fair, maidenly visage, watches me with faithful, yearning eyes. Ever new dreams and sacred ideas assume human shape! The moonlight burns in a thousand blue flames that blaze up toward the heavens like sacrificial candles, and the aroma of the moonlight night rises like incense and the forest rustles in the deep, solemn tones of an organ.

I turn away.

In the end, I am horrified by these shimmering dreams, these idealistic lies from a thoughtless youth intoxicated with life.

Reality is raw but honest. It is a lie that nature wants to know nothing of you. Eternally changing, it is unchanged and displays today the same cold, dark, but motherly face it did a thousand times a thousand years ago. You, however, have torn yourself away from her; you observe her with indifference; you are contemptuous of her children, your brothers, who are less than you; you have raised yourself above them and are now suspended between heaven and earth like the Polish Faust.[1] And yet her thousand breasts nourish her unloving son, and her arms are always open to receive him again. Her severe laws are written on bronze tablets all around us; you can read them wherever you look if you are willing to learn from her.

Again the reapers' song rang out. The grasses waved among themselves like flames. The forest rustled majestically.

I slowly undressed, inspected my rifle, placed it in the corner near my head, and threw myself into the monastic bed that stood against the undecorated wall. My dog stretched himself out, as always, in front of it, looked at me one last time with his faithful, understanding eyes, beat the floor with his tail, and then bedded his head down on his tired front paws. The rhythm of his tail became slower and slower, and his breathing became deeper and deeper, and then he sighed and dreamed. The window remained open.

I also dreamed for some time with my eyes open, and then, apparently, I slept. I was tired, and there soon came over me that pleasing forgetfulness that is a friendly precursor of death.

I don't know how long I lay there.

Suddenly I heard a strange noise, first while half asleep, then clearly, with my eyes wide open. The dog roused himself, lifted his beautiful head with its watchful eyes, inhaled, and then started barking hoarsely and rapidly, as if at some big, wild animal. I had come completely awake, and I had unconsciously put my hand on the cold barrel of my rifle.

There was a deep stillness in nature that seemed to be breathing sadly and hesitantly, and then the strange, uncanny sound again, a ghostly floating, a rustling as if from clothing dragging on the ground.

And then—suddenly—a tall, white figure was standing at the open window. A woman with a queen's stature, barely veiled by her light, billowing garments, her face turned away from me, appeared in the cold light of the full moon as if transparent. Her outstretched hand was illuminated as if by a red flame.

The hair rose on my dog's back, he shivered, slowly retreated, and whimpered. I grabbed my rifle and prepared to shoot. Even now I don't know why. It did it instinctively. My whole body was enveloped in unearthly cold.

I cocked the gun.

At that very moment, she turned her head toward me.

It was the mistress of the house. Her black, unbraided hair was flowing down over her white nightgown. Her face was even paler and seemed to glow like the disk of the moon. She smiled and gestured toward me with her hand. Only then did I see that her eyes were firmly closed. A profound shiver ran over me. She seemed to be looking through her closed eyelids into the room and at me and to be hesitating.

When I straightened up, she gestured toward me once again, put her finger to her lips, looked back once more with her closed eyes, and then entered the room. Without paying any attention to me, she slowly walked around, past me, with a firm and certain step. Finally, with her head bowed, she slowly let herself down on her knees at the foot of my bed. Her right hand rested on the bedpost, while she herself sank down and pressed her forehead against the raw wood. She lay like that for some time and then began to cry softly.

A woman's crying has never particularly moved me, but she was crying so bitterly, as if from the very depths of her chest, like an animal that can't speak, that I was shaken and bent down to her.

"He's dead, I know," she began softly with a voice that cut into my soul. "They buried him outside the wall of the churchyard like a suicide, and I want to join him." She propped her head in her hand and sighed. "But it's so far away, so far," she repeated with a dry, half suffocated sound. "And so I come here to be with him. He's here too."

Then she rose and slowly felt her way along the empty wall as if she feared that her legs might refuse to obey her at any moment. Then she suddenly turned to me, seemed to look at me for a long time, and finally shook her head. "He's not here," she said curtly and firmly. "He's dead." At the same time, her entire body began to quake, and she gnashed her teeth and threw herself onto the floor with a muffled cry, her face to the ground. There she lay, buried her hands in her hair and sobbed aloud. Then she became progressively quieter.

Finally she was completely calm.

She didn't even move.

I made a motion to come to her aid, but she sat up at that moment. Her face had become strangely tender and seemed transformed from within as if by a smile. As she rose, it was as if she was floating up slowly and solemnly, and in the end it seemed as if her feet no longer touched the ground. So softly that it was inaudible, she swam with invisible feet across the floor and then stood still facing the moon, calm, motionless, and floating in its blue light.

She looked up at the moon and spoke to me.

"What will Leopold think of Olga?" she said with gentle melancholy. She spoke of herself and of me in the third person and referred to each of us by our baptismal names. I was silent, watching her, and my heart stood still. She was obviously sleepwalking or, as our peasants say, "moonsick." I was still unconsciously holding the rifle in my hand. She came closer and reached her hand out to take it. I was startled and stepped back. A smile played mischievously around her lips. "Leopold need not be concerned," she said, "he can give Olga the rifle; she sees more than he does."

When I placed the rifle against the wall, she furrowed her brow and grabbed it impatiently, like someone who becomes angry when she's not trusted and wants to prove its unfairness. With a quick, elastic movement, she retreated and held the gun, the barrel pointing up, like a hunter waiting in a blind.

"There," she said. "There's nothing dangerous here." She carefully uncocked the gun and calmly put the gun in the corner.

I sighed with relief.

"Leopold mustn't think badly of Olga," she began, her face again turned upward toward the full moon. "Please," she cried, "I beg him," and the tears flowed once again. She knelt down and raised her arms toward me. "He must tell no one. No one at all," she continued mysteriously and softly. "Not even Olga, for she would take her own life from shame."

"No one," I said. My voice was trembling.

"No one," she repeated solemnly.

Deeply moved, I bent down toward her and wanted to raise her up. She shook her beautiful, wraithlike head and then let it slowly sink down onto her breast. "He must be told everything, everything," she murmured to herself. "Everything."

"No," I cried, "don't tell me if it causes you pain. I don't want your secret."

"He would lose his faith in Olga; indeed he is already filled with doubt," she replied sadly. "Olga is not frivolous; she is infinitely unhappy. I must tell him everything. But he has to swear. Will he?" She asked without looking up.

"Yes," I said.

Suddenly the dog crawled out and sniffed her, barked rapidly and hoarsely, and bared his teeth. She reached over to him and petted him. He trembled and shyly retreated back under the bed.

"I must, I must," she sighed. "That's the only way it can end well, the only way. "I don't want Leopold to think badly of Olga; she is so wretched." She came up to me while staying on her knees and laid her head on the bedpost. She had humbly crossed her hands on her chest like a slave. "I know he will understand Olga; that's why I'm telling him."

A slight fever shook me.

"He need not be upset," she whispered confidentially. "What I'll tell him is not a crime. Olga never intended to cause anyone any harm. Her story is simply sad, nothing more. He mustn't cry."

I leaned back against the wall and looked at her; my eyes were burning, and my mouth was quite dry.

"It will be a pleasure for me to tell him," she began with a certain melancholy grace; "he understands a woman's nature."

I nodded involuntarily.

"Olga is guilty of no sin but that she is a woman and that she was raised like women are raised, to give pleasure, not to work like a man. A woman is a peculiar kind of creature," she continued, the words flowing from her lips; "she hasn't torn herself as free from nature and is therefore that much worse and also better than a man. What people call bad and good, that is."

She smiled

"By nature, everyone thinks only of himself, and so at first, a woman discerns only usefulness and vanity in love. The first thing she has to do is live, and she can live without any effort by serving a man's pleasure; that is a woman's power and the source of her misery. Isn't it?

"Love is a luxury for her, one that a man can afford, but for her, it's her daily bread. But everyone who ekes out an existence wants more; as much as he can, he wants to elevate over others the self that he's so proudly cobbled together. A woman has her ambitions, just as a man does, but she needs only to display herself in order to find slaves and idolaters at her feet; she doesn't need to act first, to achieve, to perform like a man. She doesn't need to learn anything, either—she learns to be beautiful; what else does she need?

"And then comes the time when she learns what a man and his love are, and she is gripped by a nameless and terrifying need to love and be loved, but it is far too late by then, and her fate crashes down upon her.

"Oh, misery without hope, without inspiration, without liberation!

"Olga would have been a good wife; she has a good mind and an honest heart, but then, a woman must be educated like a man; then she'll be a companion to a man. Does he doubt that?"

I really did doubt it.

"It's not good for us when we distance ourselves from nature," I said, thinking aloud; "a woman should learn to be a good mother. Anything else is daydreaming or deception and dishonesty."

"Does he think so?" Olga replied without changing her position or the expression of her voice. "And a man's purpose would be only to provide nourishment for himself, his wife, and his child?"

"In the end, that's what it all comes down to," I cried.

"Man has changed in the course of time," she said gently. "He's left the animals far behind, and the man who thinks, plans, and invents, who has the arts and sciences, needs a different woman than the man who thousands of years ago reaped without sowing and strangled wild animals like the wolf. But let me tell him a story.

"I'll tell him everything, everything, just as it happened. I see everything so clearly in front of me, as if things had become transparent to me, and I see right into people's hearts, and I even see Olga in front of me like a stranger; I don't love her, but I don't hate her either."

She smiled in a melancholy way.

"I see her as a child."

"She was a pretty little girl with plump brown arms, dark curls, and big inquisitive eyes. Old Ivan, one of the servants on the estate who always smelled of schnaps and had red eyes as if from crying, never walked past her without picking her up in his arms and patting her gently on the leg.

"Once she was standing outside on the steps. In the house, sitting next to her mother on a worn out yellow sofa, was a young estate owner who was quite popular with the ladies. The windows were open, and she heard his voice. "She's a little Venus. You should be proud of the child. She'll be quite a woman someday." And Olga knew that he was talking about her, blushed all over, and ran into the garden. She walked quietly among the flowers, plucked roses, stock, and carnations, put them in her hair and then studied herself carefully and proudly in the little reflecting pool. A goddess of love carved of white stone stood above it. She looked up at her and thought, 'When I grow up, I'm going to be like you.'

"On winter evenings, at twilight by the big, green, flickering oven, her nursemaid, the good Kayetanova, told the children fairy tales. She would settle deeply into the black lounge chair in which the children had seen their grandfather die, and which was both venerable and chilling for them ever since. The further the twilight progressed, the more Kayetanova's friendly, rosy face sank back into the gloom, and only her blue eyes glowed in a ghostly fashion, and the more the children huddled together, the more softly they whispered. At those moments, Olga would lay her head on her nursemaid's lap, close her eyes, and see everything she heard really happen. She would always be the beautiful princess who swam across the black sea on the back of a silvery white swan or the girl carried off into the clouds by a winged horse, and none other than the Czar's son was allowed to court her, and when she once heard the tale of dumb Ivan, the peasant who wins the hand of the king's daughter, she sat up all of a sudden and cried angrily, 'I'm not the king's daughter, Kayetanova!'

"In the summer, on the other hand, when the children from the estate played under the poplars in the evening and Olga joined them, they'd play at getting married. One of the boys would pretend to be the priest. Olga had a wreath made of oak leaves and represented the bride. 'You have to be a count, at least,' she said to her little bridegroom, 'otherwise I won't marry you. I'm too pretty for the petty gentry.'

"She grew up, shot up, tall and slender, had problems with a slight cough, and thought rather highly of herself. What a great worry she was for her mother. 'Olga,' her mother said more than once, 'you're going to turn out badly; you won't get a husband, and you're going to have to live by taking in sewing like Celesta the humpback.' When the women from the neighborhood would come to visit her mother and sit around the tea table, Olga would serve, bringing out cold meat and pastries. She was a half-grown-up girl with fine lace on her little underpants and with long, thick braids down her back. Whenever the women would talk about their daughters or other girls, about their future or their material prospects, the only thing they'd think of was marriage, the same way people talk about a man's job or office.

"The pastor's daughter went to the capital and was trained to be a governess. 'Of course,' they all said, 'the poor thing is so ugly, and she's even missing her front teeth. What else could she do?' Once she came to visit during the summer, and everybody was amazed by how much she knew about geography, history, science, and foreign languages; but Olga learned only to dance, ride, sing, play the piano, draw, knit, and to speak some French—all the things that can bring a man pleasure in a woman. Nothing that could earn her a living. And then there were my mother's useful teachings: 'Don't go shifting your eyes around in your head when a man is talking to you, answer nicely, but keep it short and try to break the conversation off quickly. The more precious you make yourself, the more people will value you.' Do people talk any differently about goods for sale? She was always told that she was the prettiest girl in the whole area, and the first time her parents took her to a ball, people called her a beauty without equal. Every time she was driven to the neighbors' or to church, she was suitably dressed up, just like the horses that have ribbons braided into their tails when they're taken to market. Her mother never considered the money when it was a matter of buying an outfit for her lovely daughter. When Olga came into the room at a party, she noticed how everybody whispered, she saw the young men's glowing eyes, she heard their sweet talk and little by little, a hard, frosty cover enclosed her warm, young heart.

"The assistant schoolmaster gave Olga lessons. He had her write out rules, do sums, and read aloud. All of that was most necessary, for when she received her first love letter, she couldn't yet spell properly, and she never really learned to either. In exchange for the lessons, my parents let him live in the cramped, little house in their garden and take his meals at their table.

"His name was Tubal. I can still see him, a shy young man with big, round, short-sighted, anxious eyes, endlessly long slender hands, and a brilliant red vest that he had bought from some count's valet. But under the red vest, he had a noble, humane heart filled with love and goodness and would have been glad to sacrifice his life at any time to pull a kitten out of the water.

"When Olga would visit him in his little house, he would often be sitting on the table, mending an old shirt or his shoes; he'd always turn burning red, stutter, and run around the room as if he was looking for something. Usually he was quite pale, somewhat greenish, and covered with freckles. But as soon as Olga sat down at the table with him, he became a different man; he held a big ruler propped against his side like a cavalry officer holds his sword when he's on his horse, his voice rang out strong, and in his eyes there burned a serious, quiet fire that made Olga feel good, she didn't know why. And when she bent down over her notebook, she felt that his eyes were resting almost tenderly on her.

"Sometimes, when twilight broke in, he'd pull an old, dirty notebook from under his pillow and read Olga poetry.

"He had selected it with taste and understanding from among the best poets, and when he recited them, a sheen of enthusiasm, even beauty, settled onto his careworn face, and his voice penetrated to the depth of Olga's heart.

"On Olga's birthday, he was invited by her parents to dinner. Afterwards, they were expecting a few families from the neighborhood. There was supposed to be dancing as well. At noon, Olga went down into the garden and picked some flowers from the overflowing beds for a bouquet that was meant for the table. Suddenly Tubal was standing in front of her in white pants, a white vest, a white bow tie, and a transparent black tailcoat. His thin brown hair was combed smooth. Standing in a cloud of musk, he stammered a few verses and, trembling from head to toe, handed Olga a small package that he hesitantly took out from under his coat. Olga couldn't look at him; embarrassed, she thanked him and fled into the house where, laughing with pleasure, she threw her arms around her mother's neck. 'Tubal wished me a happy birthday,' she cried; 'he gave me a present, the poor, dear man.'

"'What could it be?' her mother replied and knitted her brow. Olga became almost frightened. 'I hope it's bonbons or something similar.'

"'Bonbons, what else could it be?' Olga said and timidly held the package out. Her mother took it, unwrapped it, and there, in the innocent white paper, lay two pair of gloves. 'Gloves!' her mother screamed. 'Yes, indeed, gloves,' Olga repeated softly, the blood rising into her cheeks.

"'Send them back immediately,' her mother ordered, 'and write him—'

"'Me write to him?' Olga said, lifting her proud head.

"'You're right. Don't write him a single word but send him back the gloves immediately. It's unbelievable. Oh, the fool! What does he think? He's trying to court my child, giving her presents or even making his intentions known to her! The whole day is ruined for me!'

"Olga packed up the gloves and sent them back to the poor tutor.

"He didn't come to dinner, excusing himself because of an illness; and he really was sick, having been consumptive for years. And so, on this day, the guests in the manor house gaily clinked their glasses, and Olga danced through the room like a bacchant while he lay on his straw mattress, coughing to the point of suffocation and using the few bread crumbs that covered his table to feed the little mouse that would come up to his bed when he was quiet and deep in thought, and the tears ran softly down his face."

The beautiful woman, who was lying in front of me on the floor as if asleep, stirred for a moment. He bosom swelled.

"I can't tell Leopold everything in the right order,' she continued. "I see too many things; the images fly past like clouds in a storm. I glimpse everything as it is, every shadow, every light, every color; I hear every sound.

"A traveling acting company on its way from Moldavia to Poland came through Kolomea and gave a few performances in the city. News of their arrival spread rapidly throughout the whole area from village to village, and on the next Sunday, when they played for the first time, almost every estate owner hitched up his horses and took his wife and daughters off to enjoy this unusual pleasure.

"The theater was set up in the large, but rather low-ceilinged room of the inn so that the actors' plumed hats kept bumping against the sky. But people enjoyed themselves wonderfully nonetheless. They presented the tragedy *Barbara Radziwilovna*.

"Before the curtain was raised, the young men stood off to the side around a middle-aged estate owner who was sitting rather casually on the window sill and swinging his legs. 'Well, where is this great beauty of yours?' he said, tugging at his mustache; 'I don't see her.' The others stood on their toes and watched the door. Finally, Olga entered the room. 'This must be the one and none other,' the estate owner said after a while. 'She's a magnificent creature!' He then went over to Olga's parents and introduced himself.

"His name had been known and respected in the whole district, and they were glad to make his acquaintance. My mother smiled up at him in her most friendly fashion, and Olga listened to him with a certain attention. At first, she was surprised by his cool certainty, but she didn't in the least think that she could love him or that he might become her husband, and yet, within five weeks, that's what happened.

"Actually, she didn't like him at all, but he impressed her, and that counts much more for a woman.

"Mihael had studied, taken long trips, and returned to his rural surroundings with a certain humor. Without making overly much of it, he talked about the actors, the play, and all sorts of things. He was capable of smiling at the saddest scenes, where Olga would cry her heart out, and all he said was, 'I'm happy to see that you're not made up. Don't you see the bloody tears that are running down the cheeks of our damsels.' And in fact, the red make-up just ran and ran down the ladies' faces when the public was choked with emotion. It was a wretchedly funny sight."

Olga's lips spread mischievously over her blinding teeth.

"After the play," she continued, "he accompanied the women to their carriage and asked their permission to visit them.

"He came and came, more and more frequently. And when he did, Olga's mother had a thousand excuses, claiming that she had things to do in the asparagus beds or that she needed to check the pantry, so that Olga was left alone with him. Mihael would talk about foreign lands, Germany, Italy; he'd been in Berlin, Venice, Florence, even in Paris, and had climbed Vesuvius and taken a sea voyage. He was able to tell about the advances being made in other nations without deprecating the abilities or the accomplishments of his own. A comforting clarity and warmth lay in everything that he said. And he was full of gallantries.

"Other women called him impolite, but when Olga dropped her knitting wool, he jumped down as fast as lightning to pick it up, and once, when he was kneeling in front of her to put her overshoes on, the blood rose to her cheeks with pleasure. People talked about him a lot. They called him a difficult, proud, strict man, but his sharp mind, his great erudition, his numerous skills, and his blade brought him uncommon respect throughout the whole district. Everyone knew that he was managing his properties according to the newest methods and that they were free of debt. He was generally considered to be the best match around.

"The more all the others watched him with a certain shyness, the sweeter it was for Olga to see this strong, active man occupied with her day and night, to see him suffer for her. She sated her pride and her virginal cruelty through him. Only when she saw the tears in his eyes was she satisfied, and then she would offer him her hand and say, 'Kiss it, I'll permit you.'

"There was a nasty, biting dog in the courtyard that always wanted to play with Olga, but would then tear at her clothes as if enraged. She kicked him whenever he crossed her path and beat him until she began to like him. That's the way it was with her husband. She abused him until she finally lay on his chest and the first kiss trembled on her lips.

"The next day, Mihael rode up in a carriage drawn by four horses. He was wearing a tail-coat and was somewhat pale. In a few minutes, everything had been settled, and Olga was his fiancee. She thought it had to be that way—she would be brilliantly cared for, and people envied her. That was enough for her.

"One evening she was sitting with Mihael downstairs by the window and sewing some things for her dowry while he talked about the future of the Slavs. Suddenly Tubal was standing before them, pale as a ghost, his eyes jutting out of his skull and the blood streaming from his mouth all over his shirt and clothes and onto the floor.

"'Salt! Salt!' he cried; he couldn't say anything more.

"Olga ripped open the drawer of the buffet and gave him salt. Mihael jumped out the window and rushed off to help the poor schoolteacher; he threw his arms around him and kept putting salt into his mouth. Tubal gulped it down greedily, but with difficulty, yet the blood kept coming. Mihael carried him to the nearest bench, and Olga brought water. Gradually the bleeding stopped.

"Tubal lay there, his eyes closed, like a dead man.

"'Put him in bed,' said Mihael; 'we need a doctor.'

"He set off on his horse himself and rode into the little town. During the night, he returned with the doctor. We had taken Tubal back to his little house in the garden, and he died there several days later. Only when he felt himself near to death did he call for Olga.

"She came, but he was no longer capable of speaking; only his lips moved, and there was a strange rattling in his chest. The gardener, who had been taking care of him, was sitting outside on the wooden steps and, with some pleasure, was already trying to see if the dying man's white pants would fit him.

"No one was with him but Olga, and she looked around carefully and then bent down over him and kissed him on the forehead, where the sweat stood in cold drops for the last time. His eyes began to shine, he stretched his hands across the blanket, and a blissful smile suddenly lay on his emaciated face. He died with this smile.

"Under his pillow, we found the little yellow notebook with the poems and two pairs of fine woman's gloves in a half-shredded bit of paper.

"Olga took both things. She still has the gloves. She wore one pair on her wedding day.

"Tubal was buried, mourned, and forgotten. The earth lay lightly upon him. Not long after that, Olga left her parents' home as Mihael's wife, who proudly brought her here to his residence in a carriage and four.

"Olga was quite happy for some time. At least that's what people believed, and she believed it herself. Like all women, she thought the world was arranged for her pleasure, a good table, beautiful clothes, horses and carriage, a sofa, cigarettes, novels. And men? They're there, she thought, to pay for our pleasures, to while away the hours, or, at most, to find us beautiful and to kneel with admiration before us. Her life floated so casually past, one day like the next. Then she had children, who soon provided her with sufficient occupation. And so she felt rather satisfied for years. After all, she didn't know anything else. Her heart was quiet, dead. Just sometimes, when she read poetry—which happened rarely—did a light begin to flicker in her soul, a nameless yearning, a disquiet that she didn't understand, and then her blood rushed, and she was feverish down into the tips of her fingers.

"And yet, things would never have changed if her husband had understood how to give constant nourishment to her vanity.

"Doesn't he believe that?"

She laughed mischievously and turned toward me. Her eyelids were fluttering, and the voice with which she spoke was that of a trusting child, and in spite of her closed eyes, it seemed to me that she had fixed me with a penetrating stare, and I had to lower my gaze.

Olga rose and, without her feet seeming to touch the ground, walked slowly to the open window, where she stood looking at the full moon. She had charmingly tilted her head back, and her arms had sunk to her side. She stood completely in a warm, glowing shaft of light, the aroma and melody of the night enveloped her, and a breath of air rustled through her hair and slid down her nightgown.

"I'd love to fly," she said after a while with a hint of embarrassed yearning. "Has he ever flown?"

"Me?"

She emitted a childish laugh. "In a dream, you know?"

"In a dream, of course."

"Then he must know how blissful it feels to glide in the quiet, clear air, the clouds drifting about us and the sea and land lying in a solemn twilight beneath us. I'd love to fly!"

She spread her arms, and the wide white lace of her sleeves fluttered at her shoulders like the brilliant wings of a cherub.

The most impossible things seemed possible to me at that moment. I ceased thinking.

"Why don't you fly?" I asked.

"I could," she replied with undescribable sadness, "but Olga won't let me."

I shivered.

"A peasant is crossing the footbridge on the other side of the grove," Olga suddenly cried animatedly. "He's going to set traps for the blackbirds that Olga likes so much. Can't he hear him?"

"No."

"It's too far away. But it's just as I said."

"Do you want to continue telling me your story?" I asked after a rather long silence.

"Yes, I like talking to him. It makes me feel so free. In his presence I see everything so clearly, and my lips move as if of their own volition and tell him what is in my soul."

"And how is it possible for you to narrate so coherently, with such detail?" I asked. "How can you describe everything so minutely, every word, every tone of voice, every movement, while seeming attentive and indifferent at the same time, as if it had nothing to do with you?"

Olga shook her head. A smile flew across her face. "It's not about me," she said simply. "I'm talking about Olga. I see Olga as I see other people, and it's all as if it were happening right now. He can't understand me. Space and time have disappeared for me, and the past and the future are spread out before me like the present. And I see everything simultaneously. When I see Olga sunk in the pillows of her ottoman and engrossed in a French novel, I can also see her breath rustling the marten fur on her jacket, and the greenish gold fly buzzing around her hair and the spider lurking on the ceiling."

Olga leaned back on the window frame, her arms entwined around her neck.

"Shall I continue?"

"Please."

"What I see now is so sad," she went on. "Olga is no longer happy.

"Her husband loves her and guards his happiness with boundless distrust. He wants his wife completely for himself, for himself alone. He's driven all his friends away. He'll tolerate no strange skirts in the house, as he puts it. He hates all the verbosity that goes with talking about people and things, books and politics, all of it with people whom we don't understand, and who will never understand us. He lives only for his wife and children; he works for them and strives to teach and entertain them.

"But his young wife begins to find herself terribly lonely in the dimly lit manor with the gloomy poplars. There's a thorn in her proud, vain heart, and she pushes it in deeper and deeper, and she wounds herself until she's incurable.

"They used to call her the best dancer, and that flattered her. When people remind her of that now, it only hurts her. Who should she dance with? Sometimes she takes her youngest child on her arm, hops around with him and warbles, and the tears suddenly spring from her eyes.

"She draws from nature, combining and inventing, sketching scenes from the books that they read together. Her husband studies them for a long time with an examining eye and then only says, 'It's good, but I'd have done it this way.' And the more he's right, the more irritable she becomes.

"She's sitting at the piano, playing Mendelssohn, Schumann, Beethoven, but for whom? She sings Schubert songs, the magnificent serenade, but who listens? Maybe a peasant returning home from the fields will stop under her window or maybe her husband is back from the fields, smoking his cigar on the divan.

"She is beautiful, and as a woman she becomes more and more beautiful. Her face is more ethereal, filled with character, more harmonious, and her body takes on a truly regal form. For whom? Her mirror praises her, but no one else. It doesn't occur to her husband to do so. Isn't his love, his complete devotion enough?

"She dresses tastefully. For whom? For the peasant woman who brings the mushrooms? For the gamekeeper who follows the master and carries the wild ducks he's shot? For her children's nursemaid? For the husband in whose eyes that's just the way it should be? He's paid for her dearly enough, after all, with his fortune and his freedom. He wants a beautiful wife, and he loves a luxurious comfort in his house and in her. It is her duty to be beautiful and he doesn't consider it an accomplishment when she heightens her charms by means of her toilette.

"She is aristocratic when she rides, jumping boldly over ditches and hedges, but who admires her? Certainly not her husband. He'd just despise her if she were cowardly. On the contrary: he reminds her to think of her children.

"So she feels like an actor who is expected to act without an audience and ends up gnashing her teeth in rage and crying into her pillow during her sleepless nights.

"One day her husband notices a cloud on her brow that doesn't seem to want to go away so quickly. 'You are so melancholy,' he says after a while. 'I've thought of something new that might amuse you.' He smiled and brought Olga the most delightful little rifle, which had just arrived from the city at his order. 'You should learn how to shoot and go hunting with me. Would you like that?'

"Everything was instantly forgotten. Olga threw her arms around him in jubilation and kissed his rough cheeks. 'I want to learn immediately,' she cried, 'today!'

"'Then today it is, the moment you give the order.' Mihael was always very gallant.

"'This very morning,' Olga pleaded.
"'Of course, just get dressed.'
"'Or now, right now,' she said shyly, 'but you won't have enough time.'
"'I always have time for you,' her husband said, kissing her on the brow. Olga fastened her white morning dress with a pin over her heaving breast and then hopped down the front steps on his arm. It was a fresh, warm morning in June, the dry air filled with the balsamic smell of hay; the earth was swimming in the hot, yellow sunlight and softly curled up into small white clouds. On the street leading past the manor, a noisy band of cheerful sparrows was bathing in the dust.

"Mihael looked at the little rifle, put it to his shoulder, and aimed; then he put it in Olga's hand, pressed it against her cheek, and gently laid her finger on the trigger. Olga aimed at an apple peeking out of the green foliage and then at a swallow that was flying along the ground. 'All right. Now watch how I load it.' Olga followed the cartridge and the ramrod with eager attentiveness. 'Now you put the capsule on. Careful. Now pull back the cock. Good. Take the apple there as your target.' Olga put the gun to her cheek.

"'Higher.'

"The shot rang out, and the leaves flew. 'Now load it yourself. It will go better the next time.'

"Olga grasped the small cartridge, shook the powder and the shot into the barrel, and firmly set the stopper on top of the capsule.

"'Do you see the sparrows over there on the street?' asked Mihael, who had been looking around with a searching eye.

"'Yes.'

"'Well, try your luck.'

"Olga didn't take a long time to think about it and aimed at them. The little creatures were chattering and swimming with their wings spread wide in the fine, white, warm dust without a care in the world, their gray heads diving in and resurfacing noisily, fluttering up into the air, squabbling, twittering, and tumbling comically all over each other.

"Then the barrel flashed. A cry rang out from more than twenty small throats, a thick swarm rose sluggishly, flew toward the hedge, and settled down on it so that the upper branches of the latter bent toward the ground. Olga shouted for joy and ran over. Five of the little creatures lay shot to bits on the ground. Their blood colored the dust. One was still twitching, turning like a top, and then it lay still, breathing its last, next to the others. Olga quickly wrapped them in her gown and flew back. 'I shot five of them, five!' she cried with a child's boisterousness, 'here they are.' She ran up the steps to the house, placed them one next to the other in a row on the landing like they place the corpses of the fallen soldiers on the battlefield before they bury them, and studied them with great satisfaction.

"'Five with one shot,' she said, still cheerful, 'that was a good shot.' Mihael loaded the rifle again.

"Olga had fallen silent in the meantime. She put her head in her hand, stared without moving at the dead little beings, and slowly, her big, bright tears fell down onto them.

"'What's the matter?' her husband shouted. 'I think you're crying!'

"Olga began to sob. 'The poor things,' she cried, 'how sad they look lying there, their feathers sticky with blood, their eyes dull, still warm. What did they do to us? I'm sure they have babies in their nests waiting for them, and they could starve, and I took away their lives and can't give them back to them! It's the fault of our own cursed lives, this loneliness! From pure boredom, people become predators.'

"Her husband laughed. His laughter sounded dreadfully raw and primitive to her at a moment like that.

"'You don't want to understand me,' Olga shouted, 'so I'll have to speak more plainly with you. It's been on my mind for a long time. Things can't go on like this unless you want to destroy me. You chase everyone away from me; you lock me up; any peasant's wife has more freedom than I do. I can't go on like this. I'm desperate. I'm going to fall ill or go mad.' She again broke into convulsive sobs.

"Her husband was silent, shot the gun empty, and then calmly went up into the house. She followed him and stood at the window, her arms crossed in front of her chest. 'You haven't said a word,' she said after a while. 'You seem to think I'm not worth the effort!'

"'I never speak without thinking first,' her husband replied. 'Have you also considered what you said to me?'

"'Considered? Olga cried. 'I've spent whole nights crying and praying to God to release me.'

"'Something will have to be done,' her husband said drily.

"'Then do it.'

"'You don't feel happy in your house, with our isolated way of life?'

"'No.'

"'You can't stand it any longer?'

"'No.'

"'You should be allowed to live as you please. Receive visitors, invite your friends, visit the neighbors, dance, ride, hunt with the others. I have no objections to that.'

"'I thank you,' Olga said, ashamed.

"'Don't thank me,' her husband replied seriously.

"'You're angry,' she said anxiously and dried her tears.

"'I'm not angry,' he answered, took her head in his hands, kissed her and then got on his horse and rode off to oversee the trees that were being cut down.

"In a short time, Olga had turned the whole house inside out. The Kolomea district seemed to consist of a single party, one big salon where people enjoyed themselves in the most exquisite manner, and she, of course, was its center, the young, beautiful woman who greedily drank in this new life with great gulps.

"The lonely estate acquired sound and color all at once; even the rustling of the great poplars seemed friendlier. The meadow shimmered with the light-colored women's gowns, gaudy hoops and badminton cocks flew up into the air, and mischievous laughter rang out throughout the garden.

"Slowly the leaves on the trees turned red. The wind swept mightily through the stubble in the fields, the summer's ribbons fluttered on the bare bushes like little flags, and cranes flew in their triangular formations toward the south. Olga thundered across the barren fields on a milky white Ukrainian horse, her cloak flying and a waving feather on her coquettish cap. The young estate owners and the women in their fantastic costumes would follow her on bold horses. The hunting horn rang out. The hare in the field lifted its long, furry ears in astonishment and then fled into the forest. The fox uttered its hoarse bark and forced its way into the bushes off to the side.

"Then the sky became grayer and grayer, more foggy, the ravens circled around the old poplars, and at night, the wolf's eyes glowed like green flames behind the fence. One cold, sunny morning, a white cover would lie thick and fluffy upon the broad plain, little diamonds sticking to the windows, water dripping from the trees and roofs, and the sparrows crying on the threshing floor. In a few weeks, the snow would stay on the ground, the sleigh with its dusty swan-head taken out of the shed, and the bearskins beaten under the cossack's whistling cane. The fire roared in the mighty Renaissance fireplaces. From all sides, the sleighs would shoot toward the hospitable manor like birds of prey, their little bells ringing far out into the flat land. In the foyer, furs were piled upon furs. The ladies would slip out of their warm, soft wrappings into the warm salon and light their cigarettes; the gentlemen, with great effort, would pull the kid gloves off their stiff fingers. Then someone would sit down at the piano and within a few chords, the couples would be lined up to dance. And so it would go from week to week, from manor to manor. The gaming tables wouldn't even be put away. The smoke drifted up from the long pipes and the empty bottles stood in the cellars in large squares like the old guards at Waterloo.

"And when, in the pale light of morning, Olga, enveloped in the dark, Siberian sable and the soft furs of the sleigh, returned home, the cossacks would ride out ahead of her with torches, from which the pitch would continually drip into the hissing snow, and all the other sleighs would accompany her as if she were a monarch.

"And she really did rule without restraint in the merry group. She was brilliant, triumphant, happy. People were already beginning to consider a man her lover if he knew how to offer her her beloved candies in an especially gracious and original way and consequently enjoyed the reward of being allowed to put on or take off her fur boots or hold the stirrup for her, whereas she had barely betrayed her husband with a word or a look. She had never treated her husband in such a friendly manner, and she strove to repay him with a hundred little gestures of tenderness. But the whisperings of society, the neighbors, and the servants also reached his ear. He trusted his wife, but he clung to his honor, and every drop of calumny that splattered onto Olga ate into his soul like poison.

"He became ever quieter and colder. When someone came to visit, he'd quietly go out the back door. More and more rarely did he accompany his wife on her excursions. In the spring he joined several other Russian estate owners and formed an agricultural club and undertook a series of improvements on his property, subscribed to several newspapers, bought a lot of books, began gathering the peasants around him and started visiting the taverns in the villages since he was thinking of running for election to the district parliament. When the harvest was past, he hunted frequently, alone, with only the dog for company. He would often not return home until late at night. Olga was in bed, but she wouldn't close her eyes and would wait for him with an anxiously beating heart. But he thought she was asleep and would quietly go off to his room. And she had never found him as interesting as she did now. Everything that he did acquired a larger significance for her. When he was away, she'd look at the newspapers that he had read and leaf through his books.

"She now began to sense what love was, and she felt that she could love her husband.

"Then, when she meant so little for him that he could talk for hours to the peasants who visited him, always leaving such a terrible reek of leather behind them, while hardly being able to find a word for her; when she spent long evenings sitting next to him without his looking up from his book; when he could go to bed without kissing her; that's when she started feeling an intense need for his love. She came up with charming negligées, and she flirted with him as if he were one of her most intoxicated admirers. He had to love her. She wanted him to love her.

"She tried everything and resolved to use desperate means.
"She decided to make him jealous.
"But where could she find the man who could agitate this cool, smart, secure man ? Olga searched in vain, but she found none worthy. Restless, she wandered aimlessly through the house and through society.

"Once her husband was standing at the garden fence, gloomily watching the sun setting behind the forest and covering with a liquid red the last ears of grain standing on the cut fields, the grasses, and the leaves on the trees. Unexpectedly, she threw her arm around him and grasped his warm, dry hand, which immediately turned icy cold.

"'Why won't you stay where I am,' she asked, yielding to him completely. 'You avoid me. Am I no longer right for you? What to you want me to do? Do you still love me?'

"Mihael stroked her cheek and looked off again into the landscape. Olga embraced him passionately and pressed her mouth against his. Her husband gently pulled away from her. 'You'll be riding off to the hunt with the master of the Zavala estate. Do you want me to accompany you?'

"Olga looked at him in shock. 'That wasn't it.'

"'Yes, it was," he said smilingly. 'Come, it's getting cool. Let's go indoors.' And once inside, he pulled Olga onto his lap and covered her neck, her lips, her breast with kisses. Her heart stood still with jubilation. Suddenly he said, 'Light the lamp and bring me the newspaper.' His wife clenched her little fist and cried all night until morning came.

"Her eyes were still wet when he helped her into the saddle. She gave him a strange look, whipped her horse, and dashed off ahead.

"The day was clear and mild. The hunt thundered merrily across the barren fields. The shooters were scattered throughout the wood, and her husband had his blind deep in the thickets. The beautiful, triumphant woman with the broken heart, her eyes filled with tears, led the hunt. She discovered the first hare that tried to save itself by fleeing from the brush into the open, and she pointed at it with her small, trembling hand. The greyhounds were let loose, the horns rang out, and with a wild cheer, the riders followed the desperate animal. She jumped across ditches, streams, and fences and laughed, filled with contempt for life. Every nerve in her body trembled with the cruel pleasure. She laughed like a child that watches a ball fly through the air when the greyhounds finally tossed the animal, screaming with the fear of death, into the air. In all eyes, there was admiration for the bold horsewoman. Her vanity celebrated a new orgy, and it was, of course, only a poor hare that breathed its last at her feet. The cavaliers kissed her sweat-soaked gloves and swung their caps in the air. With deeply flushed cheeks and sparkling eyes, she looked around the circle of hunters.

"Off to the side, on the edge of the forest, stood a young man whom she had not noticed until now. He was watching her with a peculiar earnestness and was silent.

"'Well, sir,' she arrogantly shouted to him, 'how do you like me?'

"'I don't like you,' he answered drily.

"With a quick turn, Olga brought her horse closer to him. 'And why, if I may trouble you for an answer?' she asked, more curious than hurt.

"'A woman who delights in the death struggles of an animal has to be either completely heartless or completely unthinking.'

"At that moment, something like hatred, demonic, terrifying, indomitable, grasped the soul of the poor, vain woman, but it was a different feeling. Dumbstruck, she stared at the young man.

"He would have enough substance to torment her husband. She knew that now. After all, she didn't need anything more. And he dared treat her with indifference—he'd have to pay for that. She didn't continue her questioning.

"He was the first man to speak to her like that, to treat her brusquely, almost with hostility.

"And yet there lay so much goodness in his eyes.

"She was feverish with the desire for revenge, whereas he barely took notice of her and shortly thereafter engaged in lively conversations with others at the table and in the ballroom. As far as he was concerned, she wasn't even on the same planet, and she saw that he played a role in society. She had never before felt so uncomfortable.

"She learned that he was a certain Vladimir Podolev, a man who was much spoken of at the time and greatly respected by everyone.

"'Vladimir was rude to you," said the mistress of the house, a beautiful and intelligent woman who, having been born a peasant girl, became the wife of the master of Zavala. "It's his way. He has unusual manners. On the other hand, he's really an unusual man. He sees everything differently than we do, more deeply and penetratingly. It seems that his mind can see through anything. You'll learn to think better of him. Why don't you go and talk to him?'

"And the proud woman, who rarely rewarded avowals of devotion with anything more than a contemptuous twitch of her eyebrow, walked up to him and spoke first.

"'You insulted me,' she began with trembling, pale lips. Then she had to stop and catch her breath.

"'The truth always hurts,' Vladimir replied, 'but it is healthy and does incomparable good in healing a sick soul.' And as he spoke, his eyes pierced her heart.

"'You made the comment,' Olga continued with a muffled voice, 'that I seem not to think very much. I've thought about what you said. Explain it to me. I don't understand you.'

"'How should I explain myself to you?' Vladimir asked indifferently.

"'Do you believe that man has no right to kill animals?' Olga asked, her eyelids twitching with sarcasm.

"Vladimir smiled. 'A truly feminine logic,' he said. "I wasn't talking about killing, but about hounding and tormenting.' In general, one shouldn't talk about rights in this world; necessity is all that matters, for it rules everything. In the end, man must live and kill in order to live. If he lives off plants, he kills them, too, for even the plants have life. He must kill animals, but he should do no more than is necessary, he shouldn't torment them, for animals have a will, feelings, and a mind like we do. They think, if not as sophisticatedly as we do, and to delight in their torment is not much better than slaughtering gladiators in the circus. A woman who can hound an animal to death seems to me to be no better than one of those cruel Vestal virgins who held so many lives in their hands and who so enjoyed turning their thumbs down. Eventually, a woman like that won't even shy away from human victims, for the little bit of rationality that differentiates us from animals doesn't count for much in woman anyway.'

"'I thank you,' Olga said after staring off into space for a short time. 'But let's amuse ourselves now.' And without further ado, she took Vladimir's arm and had him take her back into the ballroom. Afterward, when he was standing at the door while she was whirling past in the arms of another man, a warm, sunny glance from her languishing brown eyes would meet his eyes. Every time it was her right to choose, she chose him. She strove again and again to capture him in a net of conversation, but he always remained calm and unresponsive.

"On her way home, Olga wrapped herself sullenly in her fur and rolled up like a spider whose net has been torn.

"'Who is this boy anyway, this Vladimir Podolev?' she spat the question out with an indescribable disdain a little while later.

"'He's a man, for a change—that's all there is to say,' Mihael replied, incapable of jealousy. 'He has an estate on the Russian border and has leased a large property here in the area. He's always working, has been abroad, and has learned a lot. He's not lazy nor does he waste his time making plans, and above all, he's not vain, not a ladies' man like the rest of our young gentlemen.' He watched Olga as he spoke.

"'Vladimir isn't Polish?'

"'How can you even think that? Have you ever met a Pole who learned anything worthwhile? He's a Russian. That's obvious.'

"And that poor, arrogant woman spent that whole night brooding about how she could capture that contemptuous boy. The next morning, Olga rose from her bed with the decision to make him her prey. She didn't ask whether he would suffer during the course of the hunt. It brought her pleasure, and so he was to be surrounded with nets and then pursued like a fox.

"But that wasn't so easy.

"A few days later, Vladimir came to visit her husband. Olga flattered herself that he was coming for her sake and walked up to him with a smile that was filled with triumph. 'My husband is in the village and won't return until late,' she said, expecting that Vladimir would somehow betray his pleasure in the news. Instead, he said quite bluntly, 'Then I'll come tomorrow.'

"'Why don't you stay here with me?' she asked in astonishment.

"'I rode over to see how he manages the estate, and you can't show me that,' Vladimir replied.

"'Well, then keep me company.'

"'I can't do that,' was his answer. 'You wouldn't find me amusing, and my time is too precious to spend inflating empty phrases. Life is so short and there's always a lot to do and to learn. Farewell.' And with that he was gone.

"He returned the next afternoon. Olga was reading a new French novel and didn't move from her rocking chair. He was talking with her husband in the adjoining room. The door wasn't completely closed; she didn't want to listen, and she stared at her book, but she didn't miss a word. With irritation, she recognized how truly, intelligently, clearly, and succinctly Vladimir always spoke. He wouldn't touch a topic in which he wasn't well-versed. In his manner of speaking, things and people seemed transparent. Her husband said repeatedly, 'There are things I can learn from you, my friend!' She knew what that meant, coming from him.

"It had gotten completely dark before Mihael called her name, whereupon she appeared at the door with a certain haste. She could see only their cigars swimming in the darkness like little, fiery circles, but she nonetheless noticed that Vladimir rose to greet her, for his cigar floated quickly upward like a lightning bug.

"Mihael asked for tea. When the cossack had set the small table and set up the lamp and the hissing samovar, Olga appeared, returned Vladimir's greeting with a slight nod of the head and sank into the nearest little chair. The cossack served them a cold repast. Olga filled the cups, lit her cigarette over the lamp, and leaned back. The men then continued their conversation unperturbed while she watched the blue smoke, which slowly dispersed in ever broader circles while she observed Vladimir through the dark lashes of her half-closed eyes.

"He wasn't handsome, but rather what you would call interesting—not ugly, either—nor really young; younger, perhaps, than she was, of medium height, slender, almost fragile, with small hands and feet, but his posture and his movements had something exceptionally energetic about them. His long, gaunt face didn't betray the least trace of redness, but it was more weathered by the sun, severe, and brown than pale. The rather low brow revealed striking ridges above the strongly bent nose and eyes. Olga felt tempted to look him up in Gall's typology of skulls. Over the sharply drawn chin, a full, upturned mouth displayed two rows of flashing teeth. Vladimir didn't wear a beard and had thick brown hair that he combed straight back like a German pastor or teacher. While Olga was noticing all that, she avoided his gaze because anyone looking at him had to look into his eyes, which were so attractive with their calm, clear, magnetic expression: big, deep-brown eyes, whose mood was constantly changing. One moment a devilish sarcasm would flash from the half-closed eyelids, only to yield to a moist, warm brilliance under the long, silky lashes the next or, perhaps, a cold, intellectual sharpness that cut into your very soul. But always they spoke with the honesty of knowledge, that truth of the heart that brooks no doubts.

"Despite his sober and thoughtful nature, a certain poetry enveloped his whole being.

"That was the man who paid as much attention to the most beautiful woman as to a fence post.

"He was talking to her husband most seriously about agriculture, horse breeding, and the management of the forests, and later, political issues. Olga discarded her cigarette and listened.

"'Are we boring you, Madame?' Vladimir asked mockingly.

"'No,' replied Olga, 'I'm finding greater pleasure in listening to you than in our so-called conversations. We so much like to forget how impoverished and fragile our entire existence is, and how hard we have to work and to struggle. The earnestness with which you take everything does me good. I felt—how can I express this—as if I were leaving my perfumed boudoir for a pine forest where my chest expands in the fresh, sharp air.' The vain woman said all of this without any arrogance, simply, almost confidentially.

"For the first time, Vladimir looked at her sharply and for a long time, and when he left, he offered her his hand. How cold that hand was and how firm, a hand of iron."

Olga told her story so smoothly. Her voice rose and sank melodically like a murmuring spring. It almost seemed that she was reading her tale aloud with a charming lilt or that she had learned it by heart and was now reciting it. She was obviously living through everything once again, every trait, color, and sound, every movement stood before her as if physically present. I closed my eyes and just listened; I didn't even dare breathe loudly.

"Vladimir began coming rather often," she continued. "Olga treated him quite differently than she did other men. In his presence, she was modest, undemanding, she listened when he spoke, asked a few questions, and spoke little herself, but her eyes were always fixed on his. Her clothes displayed a refined, elegant simplicity; she always wore a dress of dark silk that was closed to the throat with a small, white collar. Her magnificent hair lay in thick braids atop her head like a dark bracelet.

"While other men drank from her shoe, she smothered Vladimir with a thousand little courtesies and literally courted him. Every one of his remarks seemed important to her.

"Once he pronounced a rather heavy judgment against the wearing of corsets.

"The next evening, she appeared in a comfortable kazabaika[2] made of dark velvet, lined and trimmed with marten fur.

"'That's better,' said Vladimir, looking at her with a certain pleasure for the first time.

"'I'll never again wear a bodice,' Olga quickly responded.

"'Why not?'

"'Because you've given me reasons not to,' she cried, 'and you understand things better than the rest of us.'

"At tea she accidentally brushed his fine hand with just the bristles of her fur trimmed sleeve, but she saw the electricity of that touch. Her breast rose and her eyes flashed in triumph.

"But he knew at the same moment that she wanted to conquer him and was even more reserved after that, avoided her as much as possible, and attached himself even more ardently to her husband.

"Coincidence decreed that a few days later the conversation turned to a coquettish noble woman for whom a young officer had perished in a duel.

"'You have to wonder whether such a woman has any feeling for her honor, her children,' Mihael mused, 'when she doesn't even shy away from bloodshed.'

"'Oh, the honor of this type of woman is that of a conqueror—it is measured only in successes,' Vladimir cried contemptuously. 'A woman like that will sacrifice everything to her vanity, be it happiness, love, or respect. But a man of honor and character will always steer clear of her. Only ladies' men, idiots, and knaves will be her worthless catch, just like a cat that, unable to go out of the house for a more noble hunt, will settle for mice or flies. This type, by the way, is becoming more and more common, for our educated woman has nothing better to do with her time than read novels and play the piano. It's really a disaster.'

"'Do you despise the arts?' Olga challenged him.

"'Oh, no,' he answered with feeling, 'but there is no true pleasure without work. These men who created the immortal works of art also worked; they dipped their brush or their pen in their own heart's blood. The only person who is capable of understanding and enjoying is someone who has also achieved something.'

"'You're right,' Olga replied sadly. 'How often have I felt a dreadful emptiness, a disgust toward all of life in my own breast.'

"'Try to work,' Vladimir said sternly. 'You're still young. You can still be saved.'

"Olga didn't dare look at him.

"Weeks passed. Gloomy fogs drifted around the manor house, the broad plain was again covered with deep snow, and the pond was covered with shimmering ice. The sled, however, was still standing dusty in the shed. Moths had begun to settle into shiny bearskins. Olga buried herself completely in the soft cushions of her ottoman and broods. The less Vladimir caught fire in her burning gaze, the more her arrogance demanded his subjugation. She was insulted, wounded, demeaned in her own eyes. She had to see him at her feet, and then, with the joy of a conqueror, she would walk all over him. It didn't even occur to her to think herself in any danger. She saw before her the first man who was worth conquering, and she didn't expect her charms, her beauty, her art to fail at this most crucial moment.

"No, she must have him. She was willing to pay any price for him, even the highest!

"She knew that he respected work, and so she began to work.

"'You're exercising a wonderful influence on my wife,' her husband says to Vladimir one evening while Olga sits nearby with a knitting frame. 'Look how she's been occupying herself for some time.'

"Vladimir looks at her. 'Have I told you that you should ruin your eyes and crush your breastbone? Stand up immediately.' Olga obeys. 'You have better things to do,' he continues. 'As much as I'm pleased to see you active, I miss in your house that brilliant cleanliness that distinguishes Holland and parts of Germany. There's a task that would keep you healthy and beautiful.'

"It was the earnest, iron man's first recognition of her. With surprise, Olga turned her exceedingly red, blushing face to him and looked at him with a mixture of shyness and gratitude.

"The next time she met Vladimir, she was wiping the spider webs from the ceiling of the dining room. 'That's no work for you,' he said softly. 'I didn't mean for your delicate lungs to inhale so much dust.'

"'But what should I do, then?' she said. 'My housekeepers aren't Dutch.'

"'You'll make them Dutch,' he cried. 'Just be strict and fair at the same time, but not just once, a hundred times, every day, throughout the year. Never forget that you're the mistress, that as soon as you do the work of a lazy servant, you're doing the same thing Napoleon did when he took up the post of a sleeping grenadier.'

"And with that, Vladimir led her around the whole house, including the kitchen and the cellar.

"'You'll have enough to do from morning till night if you want to supervise all of this. Instructing, giving orders, directing: that's your task. And keep the accounts, too, and that will be a significant relief to your husband.'

"From the terrace, he showed her the garden. 'When spring comes, you can sow, put out seedlings, dig, water, and weed; all of that will do you a great deal of good. And you can even be cruel here, something that every woman has to be from time to time, by waging a merciless war on caterpillars and grubs. I'd really recommend some beehives and those industrious little creatures that I love so well. And now,' he concluded as he accompanied her back into the salon, 'now let me request that you play something for me. You play with such understanding and feeling.'

"Olga's whole body trembled. She sat down at the piano, her head down, and let her fingers glide over the keys.

"'I understand your playing when I watch your fingers, these transparent fingers that seem to have their own soul,' he said quietly.

"Even Olga's lips had turned pale. She laid her hand upon her heart for a moment and then she played.

"It was Beethoven's *Moonlight Sonata*.

"At the first plangent tones of the adagio, Vladimir laid his hand over his eyes. All the magic of a moonlit night streamed over her and him; deep shadows sank down upon them, a magical, quivering, melancholy light; and their souls vibrated in harmony with the dusky, painful melody. When the last note dissolved into the air, she slowly let her hands sink.

"They were both silent.

"'Renunciation and surrender,' he finally said, 'that's what is speaking to us through this wonderful sonata. It comes as if from nature itself, from the world that surrounds us. The surrender of the heart and renunciation, whether it is a disappointed love that lives on in a faithful heart or a love that is condemned to eternal silence. We must all learn to renounce.'

"He looked at Olga, and there seemed to be tears in his eyes. He was remarkably gentle.

"He avoided coming for some time. Olga understood him.

"Then came a day on which her husband went off to Kolomea, the district capital, to make some purchases. She stayed behind. Her heart threatened to stand still at any moment. She knew that he would come, and when the first shadows of twilight fell into her room, she quickly slipped into her fur-trimmed kazabaika and sat down at the piano. Almost involuntarily, she began the sonata. She ended abruptly with a dissonance. She was steaming with heat in the voluptuous fur, so she tore it off and paced vigorously back and forth , her arms crossed under her heaving breast.

"And then he was standing in the room.

"The blood shot into her cheeks. She pulled the kazabaika around her, and gave him her hand.

"'Where is Mihael?' he asked.

"'In Kolomea.'

"'Then I'll — '

"'You're not leaving?'

"Vladimir hesitated.

"'Since early morning, I've been looking forward to speaking with you, alone,' Olga said in a muffled voice. 'Please, stay here with me.'

"Vladimir laid his cap on the piano and sat down in one of the brown fauteuils. Olga took a few more steps through the room and then came to a stop in front of him. 'Have you ever been in love, Vladimir?' she asked quickly and bluntly. 'Oh, of course you have.' Her lips trembled with contempt.

"'No, I haven't,' he replied with the utmost earnestness.

"Olga looked at him, speechless.

"'And are you capable of loving?' she asked hesitantly. "I don't believe you are.'

"'Again, you are wrong,' Vladimir answered. 'Natures like mine, which should not be spent in small coins and which have matured without flirting and playing, may be the only ones that are capable of truly loving. How should an unripe, green plum of a girl or boy be capable of it? Only a man can truly love. Perhaps a woman also, but most of them have already given away their hearts in bits and pieces.'

"'And what would a woman have to be like for you to love her?' Olga continued without moving from the spot.

"Vladimir remained silent.

"'It is of particular interest to me,' she murmured.

"'Must I answer?'

"'Please.'

"'Well, she would have to be the exact opposite of you,' he said drily, his voice strained.

"Olga became as pale as death, and then the blood rushed to her cheeks and the tears to her eyes. She looked silently at the floor.

"'Well, laugh,' cried Vladimir with melancholy humor, 'it must seem infinitely laughable to you.'

"'You aren't courteous,' Olga replied, her voice smothered with tears.

"'But honest,' he responded mercilessly.

"'You have an antipathy toward me,' Olga said firmly, throwing her head back arrogantly at the same time. 'I've sensed it for a long time.'

"Vladimir fired off a short, hoarse, endlessly sad burst of laughter. 'Well, then, I'll tell you the whole truth,' he cried with intense bitterness. 'I feel more for you than for any other woman on earth.'

"Olga looked at him in shock. Her heart was beating in her throat and her blood was ringing in her ears.

"'I could love you,' he continued more calmly with a look filled with painful devotion.

"'Then do. Love me!' Olga cried.

"'No,' he said softly, 'first there would have to be respect.'

"Olga gestured with incomprehension.

"'Please, don't misunderstand me,' he continued. 'I don't want to hurt you. I simply want to explain myself to you. At its most essential, it is just an inborn drive that brings people together, just as it is with animals, but it is not a drive divorced from choice. The whole thing isn't about us, it's about our race, not our pleasures, but a new life. Every day is the day of creation. Instinctively men and women seek in each other those characteristics that they lack, that they respect or love the most, and this selection becomes more and more individual, more astute, the more human reason plays a role in it. True love, therefore, can only arise from a powerful, innate drive, a magnetic instinct, but it can only last by virtue of a complete and mutual respect for each other's character and habits. If I've gone too far afield, go ahead and laugh at me!'

"'I'm not laughing,' Olga replied darkly. 'And so you don't feel that respect for me.'

"'Not that complete respect,' Vladimir interrupted her, 'that I demand if I'm to devote my heart and my life to one woman.'

"'You despise me,' Olga said angrily, and her temples began to throb.

"'No, I pity you,' Vladimir replied. 'I'm involved with you in the most intimate fashion. I think about you often and would like to save you.'

"'Why do you despise me?' Olga screamed from the depths of her soul. 'Tell me, I want to know!' At that moment, she angrily set her foot on his chair with a certain wildness, and her eyes sparkled with hatred and murder.

"'All right, then listen to me,' Vladimir said with an icy coldness. 'You are a woman of rare beauty, a strong mind, a gentle and tender spirit, a woman who was created to make the very best man her slave. Does that satisfy you? No! You want to celebrate a new victory every day, to rest on fresh laurels every night. Your vanity is insatiable, and it eats at your heart like a vulture, but this poor little heart doesn't grow back like the titan's, and so you will end disgusted with life, hating other people, and despising yourself.'

"Olga let out a groan and then began to cry loudly, to tear at her hair, and to grind her teeth. When she raised her arms, her fur fell open, and she stood there with an angrily heaving breast and blazing eyes, her black hair undone, and raging at him like a maenad.

"Vladimir stood up.

"She forced a painful cry from her lips and lifted her clenched fists.

"He only furrowed his brow and looked at her, whereupon her hands fell to her sides and her head sank down on her breast.

"A moment later he was gone, and she was lying on the carpet sobbing.

"Days passed, weeks, a month.

"Vladimir didn't return.

"He also avoided her husband.

"Olga suffered terribly. She now knew that he loved her, but she also knew that he despised her, and her passion was ignited both by his attraction and his hatred. She began a letter and tore it up. She had her horse saddled in order to go to him, but she didn't go. She would stand in the kitchen for hours and stare into the fireplace. A feeling that she had never experienced before came over her. She thought only of him. When she stood at the window in the twilight, she expected to hear his horse, his step, his voice at any moment. She tossed and turned night after night, sleepless, on her bed and would find slumber only toward morning.

"She now understood music and poetry for the first time.

"It had gotten dark. She was sitting at the piano and playing the *Moonlight Sonata*, and her tears flowed with the music. Her husband quietly walked up behind her and pulled her to him. He asked nothing, and she silently laid her head on his chest and cried."

Olga's voice sank to a whisper. She had turned away from me in shame, and her entire soul trembled in chaste and profound love.

"It was Christmas Eve," she continued. "Olga was in the sleigh with her husband coming back from Tulava where he had delivered a few documents to the parish priest, and they rode past Vladimir's estate.

"A deep shiver gripped Olga when her husband unexpectedly had the driver stop at his door. 'We'll take him with us, come,' Mihael said. Olga didn't move. 'Don't you want to?' She shook her head. Her husband went in and came back with Vladimir a short time later. He greeted her respectfully and then climbed into their sleigh. No one said a word during the ride. Olga sat at Vladimir's side without moving, only shivering once when he involuntarily touched her. When they arrived, Vladimir studied the manor that he knew so well with a strange smile.

"After Mihael had helped his wife out of the sleigh and had taken off her heavy fur, he said, happily rubbing his hands together, 'We're going to have a real Christmas Eve. Let me see what the children are doing.' And with that he left the room, leaving her alone with Vladimir in the salon.

"Vladimir pressed one hand against his heart, the other against his forehead. Sobbing, she threw her arms around him with the strength that comes from despair, and the iron man began to cry, enfolded the poor woman in his arms, and, overcome, hung on her lips. The objects around them began to spin. They felt only the painful bliss of each other's heartbeat.

"Then footsteps could be heard in the next room. He let her go and walked over to the window. Olga leaned on the desk, more dead than alive. Her husband entered, stared at each of them with a penetrating gaze, and then announced that the table was ready for dinner. He said nothing, but he was quiet and out of sorts the whole evening, whereas Olga greedily drank one glass of wine after another and ran around with the children in the most boisterous fashion. Finally they lit the candles around the creche and called the servants. Two singers arrived with them, a venerable old man with a white beard and a young boy with mischievous eyes, and they sang our wonderful old Christmas carols, which are filled with melancholy and renunciation one moment and become sentimental or wildly joyful the next, just like our national character. Everyone joined in.

"And when they sang about the child who lay in the cradle and whom the shepherds greeted with reverence because he had come to save us from death and sin, Olga's voice was choked with happy tears, and she humbly folded her hands in her lap and stared at the man to whom she had yielded her soul.

"When she woke the next morning, Olga noticed that it was as if the world had changed around her. The little bit of sunlight that was lying on the floor brought her a great, childish pleasure; the snow in the garden and in the fields shimmered amiably; the ravens that were hopping over the frosty white clods of earth all looked so brilliant, as if they were dressed up for a special occasion; and in her own heart, there was a pleasant unrest.

"On the second day of Christmas, Mihael rode over to a neighboring estate owner, a Little Russian, at whose home a number of members of his political party were dining. Vladimir knew it.

"That afternoon, the light already growing dim, the bells on his horses rang out in the courtyard.

"Olga ran to meet him, then hesitated, and with averted eyes offered him her hand. Vladimir squeezed it passionately and led the enamored, trembling woman to the little brown sofa, where she pulled him down next to her. There was an almost virginal chastity in her whole being, her posture, when she laid her head tenderly on his shoulder. She was thinking of nothing else at that moment, not of herself, not even of him. She snuggled up to his chest and was happy.

"'Were you expecting me?' Vladimir began shyly.

She nodded quietly without changing her position, then suddenly took his arm and laid it around herself.

"'You can probably imagine why I've come,' he began again.

"'What is there to imagine?' she asked naively. 'I love you, and I'm not imagining anything.'

"'Doesn't your conscience tell you that we can't just go on drifting like this, making no decisions?' he asked in a muffled voice.

"'You know that I have no conscience,' she replied, and, beginning with the corners of her mouth, her mischievous smile suffused her whole face with charm.

"'My head has cooled again,' Vladimir continued earnestly. 'I've honestly weighed our situation. Everything is up to you now. I've come so that we can talk, so that we can become clear about the future.'

"'What else is there?' she replied. 'I love you more than anything. I don't want to know anything else.'

"'Olga!' he cried, almost frightened.

"'Well?' She sat up. 'Are you trying to tell me that the passion of the moment carried you away and deceived you, that you don't love me?'

"'I love you so much—you don't know how much I love you. You can't know,' he said with touching conviction, 'and that's why I truly want your happiness. You can't be happy like this. Can I allow this love that has risen above us on its own to cast you down into the filth in which I, with infinite pain, had already believed you to be mired? You weren't happy until now, but you were honest and faithful to your obligations, and you expect me to be the man who will teach you to sin, cheat, and become a hypocrite? And how will you be able to have a calm heart in your breast when you are forced to show two faces, one to your husband, the other to your lover, and not know, in the end, which one is the lie? I don't want that. I don't want you to sink. I want to cleanse your heart. I want to raise you out of these miserable whims of your vanity. I want to save you, not ruin you. Olga! Dear, dear Olga! And besides—believe me—I'm not capable of all those things that are so easy for other men. How awful that I can't ask you to be my wife. Marriage is a sacrament for us, and it seems contemptible to me to steal another man's wife behind his back, especially your husband. He means a great deal to me, and I respect him. And besides, I can't share you. I can give you up, but to call you mine and to know that the woman I love is in the arms of another—I can't do that.'

"Olga had listened to him with her eyes wide open. 'So what is it that you want to do? I don't understand you. He is my husband; after all, he has a sacred right to me.'

"'If this right is sacred,' Vladimir answered coldly, 'then we shall not transgress against it. At least I won't.'

"'Vladimir!'

"Olga exclaimed his name almost as if it were a pain emitting from her breast and threw her arms around him. "What should I do? Tell me! I'll do whatever you want.'

"'I only want us to remain honorable, Olga,' he replied, 'and to act honorably. Do you love me?'

"Olga passionately pressed her moist, hot lips against his mouth. 'Now I know what it is to love,' she whispered. 'I can no longer live without you, without your eyes, your voice. Kiss me.'

"'Don't do this,' he said, gently pulling away from her. 'More than anything else, I want the truth from you.' He stood up and walked through the room.

"'If your life depends on me like mine depends on you,' he continued, 'then leave your husband, openly, honestly, before the whole world.'

"Olga trembled. 'I can't do that,' she murmured. 'My poor children! And Mihael! He loves me so. And what would people say? My honor forbids me—'

"'I'm not trying to force you,' he said gently. 'I'm not demanding that you follow me, but you'll have to fulfill your obligations and extinguish your feelings for me.'

"'Vladimir!' Olga cried, pale and paralyzed with fear, 'you want to leave me!'

"She threw herself down on her knees in front of him and in despair, pressed her tear-streaked face against his legs.

"'Don't leave me! For God's sake, don't leave me. I'll be a lost woman without you, I'll die. I won't leave you!'

"Vladimir attempted to raise her up. She embraced him the more tightly and cried at his feet.

"'I'll always love you,' he said with a melancholy voice, 'you and none other. I'll come to visit you every day. I'll teach you the poets and the stories about prehistoric times, the flowers and animals and stars. I'll be good to your children and your husband.' He pulled her toward himself and kissed her on the top of her head.

"'If you can abandon me to him, you don't love me,' Olga murmured.

"'And am I not abandoning you to him if you become my lover but remain his wife?' Vladimir said bitterly.

"Olga was silent.

"'We must renounce our love,' he began once again.

"'I can't!'

"'You must. I won't let you fall,' he said softly. 'You know now what is indispensable to you.'

"'I know nothing but that I must have you completely!' Olga began to shout.

"'Control yourself,' he said sternly. 'I must leave.'

"'Vladimir!'

"'I must. I'll leave you time. Examine your heart, and come to a decision. Write to me then—that will be easier for you. Then I'll come again, like I used to, calm, sincere, without anger and without hope.'

"He gave her his hand.

"'You can leave without kissing me?' Olga shouted, threw her arms around him, and kissed his lips with such force that they were bleeding when she let him go. 'Go now,' she said brusquely and fixed her loosened braids. "Go! Oh, you can't go! You are really weak!'

"'Indeed I am,' Vladimir stammered. His arms enclosed her, and tears came to his eyes. 'And that's why I must leave.' He let her go and rushed out of the room.

"In the sleigh, he turned around once more. She was standing on the steps and waving to him with her handkerchief.

"Olga awaited him in vain on the next and the on the subsequent days. New Year's Eve came, and she thought he couldn't possibly stay away, but he did. On New Year's Day, a servant came with his card.

"Olga locked herself in her room and brooded, but she came to no decision. All the emptiness of life, all the doubts and pains besieged her heart.

"She asked herself in vain what she wanted. She finally stopped thinking and let herself be carried along on the waves. Nothing lay before her any longer but a great, dawning happiness.'

"The next morning she put her bare feet in her slippers and rushed to her desk. She didn't know what she should write. All she wanted was for him to come. She was being consumed by feverish yearning. She made the cossack gallop off with his horse, but he came back without an answer. Vladimir wasn't coming.

"He sat at the window of his study in his worn-out easy chair, the stuffing creeping out from all sides, the sad, silent winter landscape before him, reading a book that he called his bible, the book from which he had so often taken comfort and inspiration, Goethe's *Faust*. There was no book in his own native language that was as dear to him as this.

> 'You are aware of but one of these drives,
> Oh, may you never learn to know the other.
> Two souls, alas, dwell within my breast.'

"He understood the last line for the first time today. The night was already settling in as he leaned back, closed his eyes, and let that verse resound in his soul again and again.

"He heard a quiet sound, like something creeping on velvet paws. It must be the cat. He didn't move.

"And then, a half-suppressed, melodious laughter cascaded down upon him. When he turned around in surprise, Olga was standing before him. She took off her big, heavy fur and threw it over him.

"Before he could wiggle out from under it, she'd already gotten down on her knees and was embracing him, covering him with kisses.

"'My God! What are you doing? What risks are you running?' Vladimir cried in horror. "Get up! You must leave this very instant!'

"I'm not moving from this spot,' Olga murmured. 'I'm not afraid of anything when I'm with you.' And she enfolded him more tightly in her arms and laid her head defiantly on his knee.

"'Olga, dear Olga. I'll perish from my fear for you. I beg you, leave me!' Vladimir pleaded.

"'You've abandoned me,' she replied. 'I won't abandon you. I'll stay until the night comes, and I'll return every day.'

"'For God's sake, no!' he shouted.

"'I will come,' Olga said decisively.

"He looked at her for a long time as if he wanted to fathom her very essence. He no longer understood her. Was that the same shy, embarrassed, submissive woman?

"His head began to burn.

"'If you've come to a decision about my fate, he began with agitation, 'tell me about it.'

"Olga didn't move.

"'Tell me, please.'

"She felt his knees shaking.

"'I'm not capable of deciding between you and my children,' she replied without daring to look at him. 'Don't torment me. Give me what I'm giving you, love, and don't ask for anything more.'

"'I must, for your sake. Olga, dear, beloved Olga, answer me!' Vladimir pleaded with true fear in his heart.

"'I don't want to answer,' she said.

"'This is about you, your happiness, your conscience, the peace of your soul,' he continued.

"'You see,' she murmured, 'you despised me, cast me aside, and now you lie at my feet, and if I wanted—'

"'I insulted you and hurt you,' he said softly as if in a dream. 'Now you can walk all over me.'

"'You little simpleton!' she cried mischievously. 'What would I gain by that? Think for a moment.'

"'If I could still think,' he replied. A gentle sadness lay in his whole being. 'This one monstrous sensation consumes everything else. I've ceded to you my best thoughts and feelings, the principles of my whole life, and, like the dandelions trembling spheres, you blow them away into the air as if it were a game. I'm not asking you now what will come next. I know only that I want to be yours, your unthinking possession, your slave.'

"She made no reply. It was quiet in her soul. She now knew what love and happiness were.

"Shortly after her wedding, Olga had given her nursemaid a small leasehold, an insignificant patch of land at the edge of the estate that lay hidden in the underbrush.

"The faithful old woman, eager to be of service, was taken into their confidence, and the lovers would meet in a room of her little house that Olga secretly decorated with genuine luxury.

"Vladimir was now completely devoted to her.

"They both floated in bliss. All the pain, all the discomfort were erased from Olga's life by the feeling that lay in her innermost being and that filled the whole world with light and brilliance for her. And a deep anxiety suddenly came over her in her infinite happiness, a maidenly shame, and it touched her lover's very soul. She trembled every time that Vladimir brushed against her dress.

"It was then that this second voice began to speak in Olga for the first time. It was Vladimir's extraordinary perspective that awakened the other soul in her.

"It happened during a thunderstorm. The lights were extinguished, and the room was illuminated only by the red lightning outside. Olga lay on his chest, drunk with sleep. And suddenly the visions came, and she spoke to Vladimir.

"He didn't understand it at first and shook her arm and called her name. But she didn't wake up. A nameless horror gripped him and he listened, partly curious and partly anxious, to Olga's speeches until the clouds had passed, the thunder rumbled only in the distance, and Olga lay as if transfigured in the full light of the moon.

"Then Vladimir took heart and began questioning her, and so he asked her, 'Is there a God?'

"'I don't know anything about him,' Olga said.

"'And is there life after death?'

"'No!' Olga replied.

"The blood turned to ice in his veins, and his heart stood still.

"Olga saw this and said, 'She can see nothing beyond the atmosphere of the earth. She doesn't see what becomes of man after his death, but she is terrified of the grave, of lying in the cold earth where the worms will eat her. She would rather lie under the open sky, but then the ravens would come and devour her. Vladimir must promise to place her in a vault when she dies.'

"He promised.

"In a short time, he became accustomed to Olga's second soul and gladly listened to her talk. She loved him, too. But Olga would have given her life for him. The hours with Vladimir always passed like a blissful dream for her.

"Now Olga hated society and made an occasional appearance only so that no one would notice her absence.

"Vladimir often came to the manor house and not infrequently stayed the night. He would sleep here, in this room, in this bed, and Olga—"

She hesitated.

Now I understood everything.

"And Vladimir was so good,' Olga continued. 'He would always bring books and read to Olga, and he instructed her children with the patience of an angel.'

"When spring came, he planted the garden with Olga. There wasn't a single flower there that they hadn't planted together, and there wasn't a single head of cabbage or a single turnip that they hadn't grown themselves, and the bees sat on Olga's hands as if they were tamed canaries, and they crawled around in her hair. She also knew where every nest was in the garden, the sparrows in the old pear tree, the little finches, the nightingale, for Vladimir showed them to her, and she often watched the parents flying back and forth and feeding their fluffy babies.

"In the summer they would walk through the fields and then sit at the edge of the forest or on the terrace, the sky above them filled with stars, and Vladimir recited from memory the most wonderful things from the most diverse poets—the verses just flowed from his lips.

"Olga now started drawing landscapes and scenes from nature with great eagerness, and when she invented something, and Vladimir looked at it, and she saw in his glowing eyes that he was satisfied with it, then there was no happiness on earth that could compare to hers.

"After the harvest, they wandered through the Carpathians together. Mihael rode on in front next to the Hutsul[3] who was serving as a guide, and Vladimir led Olga's horse by its reins. They climbed the Black Mountain, saw the deep, unfathomable lake at its peak, and looked down from the highest ridges of the mountain into the endless plains of home.

"And when the winter restricted them again to the small, warm house, love seemed to them to cover the old gray walls with myrtle and roses, and the muses filled the room's intimate darkness with light and melody.

"At those times her husband would sit on the sofa with the children while Vladimir sat in one of the small brown fauteuils and Olga was at the piano. She would play the magnificent compositions of the great German masters or sing a melancholy Little Russian song with Vladimir. He often brought a book and read something aloud. Together they would read scenes from *Faust*, *Egmont*, or *Romeo and Juliette*. He was always Faust, Egmont, or Romeo, and she was Gretchen, Clärchen, or Julia hanging on his eyes and lips.

"'It's almost day; I want you now to go;
But go no further than a playful girl
Would let her pet escape her hand.'

"When the little pond froze solid, they would skate there on sunny mornings, and Vladimir taught her to cut the most remarkable patterns into the ice. When they rode in the sleigh, Olga covered his knees with her sable and put her feet on his, like on a footrest.

"But she also had dark, difficult hours.

"Sometimes she was gripped by a deep remorse, and would want to confess everything to her husband and do penance for her blissful sin. Sometimes she would have liked to run away with Vladimir and become his wife, but the children and her honor would hold her back. She vacillated and brooded and tormented herself, but when she was lying in his arms, on his loving chest, all doubts would cease, all worries, all thoughts. At those moments she would be completely happy.

"But she wasn't really happy.

"Vladimir would be silent, but she would often read his sad self-accusations from his dark brow: I'm deceiving my friend who trusts me; the woman that I wanted to elevate, I've dragged into disgrace and sin.

"She was tormented by something else.

"People noticed that her life with her husband was not going well; people pitied her, and she was so madly happy, so proud in her happiness that she would have liked to announce to the whole world: I love, I am loved by the man that you all admire, and I'm the first woman to set her foot on that proud neck.

"She had demanded secretiveness, and she was the one who couldn't bear it.

"So she herself became the betrayer of her love.

"She welcomed every opportunity to display her favor on Vladimir. He was the only one allowed to hold the stirrup for her, to lift her out of the sleigh, to help her take off her fur; she chose him as her dancing partner, demanded that he bring her refreshments, ordered him to fill her glass and to cut the meat lying on her plate. Then she'd take a bite and offer him the next on her fork, or she'd drink from his glass and give him hers, and seek the tip of his foot with hers. Her eyes were always glued to him or to the door, if he was not there yet, and as soon as he entered, she'd first turn pale and then blood red. When people talked about him, she was his most passionate advocate and spoke of his character and his mind with an enthusiasm that would make even the most inattentive and benevolent listeners take notice.

"There soon arose a buzzing, a talking, a weaving of truth, lies, and despicable behavior, and soon there was not one left who doubted that Vladimir Podolev was enjoying the proud woman's favors.

"Vague remarks made their way to her husband. For quite a long time he defended himself against his doubts about his wife, but he finally became suspicious and began watching her.

"And so a year passed.

"Spring was again casting its lovely, rose-colored light and its first white blossoms on the stairs leading up to the manor house and through the open door into the little salon where Olga was sitting at the little tea-table with her husband and her lover.

"The air was so strangely fresh and aromatic, the endless evening sky twinkling with countless stars, the quail beating its wings in the green field, and her heart felt an inexplicable anxiety and yearning, a sweet melancholy, a happiness without calm.

"Small, green-shimmering flies and white butterflies were flying around the faintly glowing glass shade of the lamp. Vladimir opened a volume of Shakespeare, and Olga looked over his shoulder and read with him:

"'All these woes—says Romeo—shall serve
For sweet discourses in our time to come.'
'O God—replies Juliette—I have an ill-divining soul:
Methinks I see thee, now thou art so loved,
As one dead in the bottom of a tomb:
Either my eyesight fails, or thou look'st pale.'

"Olga felt a strange pain in her heart, a nameless fear gripped her, and she looked at Vladimir who had, in fact, become terribly pale.

"'I can't read any more,' she stammered, 'my heart is threatening to burst!'

"'It's the spring air,' her husband said. 'Let's close the door.'

"Olga stepped outside for a moment, then returned and filled the cups. She then sat across from her lover.

"Her husband was watching her continually, and while he seemed absorbed in his newspaper, he noticed her exchanging a glance with Vladimir that was filled with a mad tenderness. At the same time, her foot touched his.

"'That's my foot,' Mihael said calmly.

"Olga started and bent over the table, trembling when she saw the terribly distorted face of her husband as he slowly left the room.

"'You've betrayed us,' Vladimir said softly.

"'I fear so myself,' she murmured. 'Now we'll have to tell him everything, and then I'll be yours, completely yours, your wife, Vladimir.'

"He looked at her with gratitude and pressed his lips against her hand.

"'Oh, how I love you! And every day and every hour more and more. You must stay here,' she continued. 'We have a great deal to say to each other.'

"'Just not tonight,' he pleaded with her anxiously. 'I have a premonition of something bad.'

"Mihael coughed before he entered, took his tea, and then complained about headache. 'Let's go to bed,' he said without emotion.

"Vladimir exchanged handshakes with him and Olga and went to his room, where he threw himself on the bed, fully dressed.

"After midnight, he could hear the rustling of a woman's dress on the terrace.

"Vladimir rushed to the window. Everything was quiet again. Suddenly, Olga jumped out of the deep shadows and threw her arms around him.

"'That was your bad premonition!' she laughed.

"Vladimir didn't reply. He helped her in, looked out suspiciously into the garden, and then closed the window.

"Olga, in the meantime, had sat down.

"'Let me live on in your memory. Farewell. For ever.

"Your Vladimir.'

"Olga silently folded the letter, stood up, got dressed, and began packing her things. She wanted to leave her husband's house immediately.

"Then she heard her children in the corridor, tore the door open, and when they threw themselves laughing and happy into her arms, she fell, sobbing, to the floor in front of them, and the suitcase stayed open.

"They found Vladimir in the little birch forest of Tulava. That is the quietest spot for ten miles around. The village's field watchman—Leopold knows him, of course—the capitulant, found him as he was patrolling the woods.

"He was lying on his back, a bullet in his chest and a pistol in his hand.

"On him, they found a letter of the type written by everyone who duels to the death. So everyone agreed that he had shot himself, and they buried him outside the wall of the churchyard.

"What's left is the everyday, the common sort of thing, but it belongs here too.

"Olga despised her husband with her whole soul, and yet she stayed with him. She was almost mad with worry. A demonic hatred often gripped her. She had already loaded the pistol with which he had killed Vladimir in order to shoot him, and yet she stayed with him because she couldn't bear not to be loved, and it did her good to see him love her, to see him suffer in the terrible feeling that she was his and yet not his.

"Her life was often quite difficult for her.

"Since that time, a deep paleness has taken over her face. Her heart is sick, and she is forced to wander in the full moon without rest!"

She was silent.

"Now Leopold knows everything," she said then with a quiet, touching humility. "Now he'll understand Olga and keep her secret."

I raised my hand as if giving an oath.

"He won't betray her, I know," she said. "Good night. The rooster has crowed for the second time, and a milky strip of light is visible in the east. I must go now."

She walked away slowly, stretching her magnificent limbs, and ran both her hands through her hair, which crackled under her fingers and threw off sparks. At the window, she turned around once again and laid her finger on her lips.

Then she was gone.

I listened for a long time and then stood up and walked over to the window. All around there was nothing but the silver of the moon flowing down onto the earth and the deep, pale silence of the night.

When I entered the little dining room the next morning, the master of the estate invited me to breakfast with him. "Then I'll show you the way back myself," he said obligingly.

"Where is our mistress?" I asked hesitantly.

"My wife is not feeling well," he replied quite casually. "She suffers badly from migraine, especially when there is a full moon. Do you know any good medicine for it, my dear fellow? An old woman recommended sour pickles; what's your opinion of that?"

We didn't take leave of each other until we had reached the far side of the forest.

Despite his friendly invitation, I avoided visiting him and every time that I pass the lonely manor house with its gloomy poplars at night, a melancholy shiver takes hold of me.

I never saw Olga again, but in my dreams her lovely image often appears to me with her pale, noble features, her closed eyes, and her unbraided, voluptuous hair.

NOTES

1. Tvardoski. Carried off into the sky by Satan, while floating over Cracow when the bells began to ring the Ave Maria, he began to sing a hymn to the Mother of God that his mother had taught him. The devil then dropped him and he remained suspended between

heaven and earth, where he can still be found today. From time to time, a spider climbs up to him and brings him news of the earth.

2. Galician woman's jacket.

3. A Russian mountain dweller of the East Galician Carpathians.

Afterword[1]

By 1869 Leopold von Sacher-Masoch (1835-1895) had reached the height of his literary fame. The success of his first novel, *Eine galizische Geschichte* (1858), later revised and reissued as *Graf Donski*, was repeated by three "Novellen" published separately in literary journals: "Don Juan von Kolomea" (1864),[2] "Der Capitulant" (The Man Who Re-Enlisted, 1868),[3] and "Mondnacht" (Moonlight, 1868).[4] The success of these works was at least partially attributable to the exotic setting in East Galicia, the ethnographic precision of his portrayals of the Ruthenians (Ukrainians), Jews, and Poles, the simple but effective realism, the serious political and social themes, and, especially in the novel, the author's attachment to his Austrian homeland.

According to an autobiographical sketch,[5] Sacher-Masoch found his authorial voice with the aid and encouragement of the eminent writer and critic Ferdinand Kürnberger. Kürnberger had rejected Sacher-Masoch's earlier work as worthless because, he claimed, it was "manufactured," like all German literature since Goethe. When Sacher-Masoch told him tales of his "Little Russian" homeland, however, Kürnberger listened "with rapture" and finally declared that if Sacher-Masoch could only write what he narrated so cleverly, he would be a true poet. Sacher-Masoch claims that he set to work that very evening and two weeks later was able to read the completed manuscript of the Novelle "Don Juan von Kolomea" to Kürnberger, who was so impressed with this work that he volunteered a foreword in which he compared his young friend to Goethe and Turgeniev.[6]

"Don Juan von Kolomea" was the first completed work to be included in the ambitious, uncompleted cycle of Novellen that Sacher-Masoch conceived under the title *Das Vermächtnis Kains* (The Legacy of Cain). Sacher-Masoch intended to portray "all of mankind's great problems, all the dangers of existence, all of humanity's ills."[7] Six groups of Novellen, each consisting of six Novellen, were to be composed on the themes of love, property, the state, war, work, and death. Of the six novellas that Sacher-Masoch planned for each of the six themes, five would explore the questions raised by the theme and the sixth would propose an answer to those questions.

The first cycle, *Die Liebe* (Love), appeared in 1870 and consisted of a prologue entitled "Der Wanderer" and, in the first volume, reprints of the three previously published "Don Juan von Kolomea," "Der Capitulant" and "Mondnacht", as well as three new works entitled "Venus im Pelz" (Venus in Furs), "Die Liebe des Plato" (Plato's Love) and "Marzella" (Marcella) in the second volume.

"Der Wanderer" articulates the philosophical framework for the entire series of six cycles in the form of a conversation between two characters: the narrator, presumably the same person in all six Novellen of *Die Liebe*, a young man of means out hunting (apparently modeled on the narrator in Turgenev's *A Huntsman's Sketches*) and the wanderer, a member of a Russian religious sect that believes the world is ruled by Satan and therefore considers it sinful to marry, own property, or acquiesce in the laws of the state, since such actions would be tantamount to accepting the authority of a corrupt world; thus, the wanderer roams ceaselessly throughout the world, always "fleeing from life."

While the wanderer's philosophy purports to mirror the Ruthenian peasant's outlook, the wanderer is in fact an emphatic spokesperson for the philosophy of Arthur Schopenhauer.[8] Although Schopenhauer's *Die Welt als Wille und Vorstellung* (The World as Will and Idea) had been published in 1819, it was only after the collapse of the the middle class's dream of political power in the conservative reaction following the failed revolutions of 1848 that Schopenhauer's pessimism became a widely accepted articulation of the bourgeoisie's resignation and retreat from the world of power and politics. "Schopenhauer made suffering the world's innermost principle—[the world became] an arena filled with tormented and anxious creatures that survive only by devouring one another" (Martini, 35), and he considered "discord, struggle, and an aimless wandering" (36) to lie at the heart of existence. Since man is driven only by the needs of his own ego, civilization becomes a "masquerade of evil" (35).

The wanderer, true to Schopenhauer's principles, rejects the concept of love, stating that men and women are, like all creatures, enemies by nature who are united only for a short time by lust and nature's blind drive to reproduce the species. Property, the state, and war arise only through the human propensity to exploit the work of others.

For Schopenhauer, the only escapes from this hell are death and art, the latter being the disinterested aesthetic contemplation of the great truths. But for the wanderer, the great keys to existence are work, the only activity that can free man from his misery, and death, which, as the only source of complete release, peace, and freedom, should be welcomed rather than feared. The narrator's reception of the wanderer's precepts seems uncritical, but its effect upon him is positive, leaving in him a "holy yearning for knowledge and truth."[9] These principles articulated by the wanderer underlie not just the remaining tales in this collection, but virtually all of Sacher-Masoch's work throughout his long career.

Only two of the projected six cycles, *Die Liebe* and *Das Eigenthum* (Property), were completed,[10] but *Die Liebe* contains what is arguably Sacher-Masoch's best work, provocative in its ideas and often startling in its succinctly powerful descriptions.

"Don Juan von Kolomea," like the other Novellen of *Die Liebe*, is a "Rahmennovelle" or novella with a narrative frame, in which the first narrator encounters the central figure of the tale, who then serves as narrator for his or her own story. In "Don Juan," Demetrius, a "Russian" (i.e., Ruthenian) estate owner, relates that his marriage was originally a happy one that provided deep satisfaction to himself and his wife, Nikolaya, until the birth of their children, when her excessive devotion to her children led her to neglect him, thus provoking the distortions in his personality that led to repeated and obsessive adultery.

The text indicates that a successful relationship between a man and a woman must necessarily be based on equality between the sexes; such a relationship was enjoyed by Demetrius and Nikolaya in the earlier, happy stage of their marriage: "Among our people, the husband has no special privileges; we have one law for man and wife." That equality, which Demetrius describes as "two monarchs negotiating with one another," is destroyed by Nikolaya's withdrawal of her affections from him in favor of her children. The inability to achieve or maintain equality between the sexes motivates many of the conflicts in Sacher-Masoch's fiction and is the basis for the repeated depiction of the mistress-slave relationship in much of his work.

The quality of the love in Demetrius' adulterous relationships is very different from the love he experienced within the marriage, as becomes apparent in his description of the peasant girl with whom he first went astray. When he first describes her, her dirty, unkempt appearance, her red scarf and the red sky behind her, her dark complexion, her hawklike nose and the snakelike hissing of her eyes all indicate a natural, passionate sensuality, but one that is dangerous and threatens to destroy its object.

Thus, while Sacher-Masoch explored uncommon forms of love with sympathy and tolerance throughout his career, his texts are often structured around nineteenth-century bourgeois values, as in "Don Juan von Kolomea," where the extramarital experience is presented so vividly and so negatively in contrast to an idealized partnership of equals within the conjugal state.

Several other aspects of "Don Juan" deserve attention. The first is Sacher-Masoch's depiction of Demetrius' personality, which, in its mixture of sophistication and naïveté, cerebral analysis and unreflected, even childish egoism, is an unusually successful portrait of the "natural" man, uncorrupted by "civilization." It was this type of living, breathing character that must have led Kürnberger to compare Sacher-Masoch to Goethe's "naïve" art, i.e., literature that seemed to arise from nature without being abstracted and attenuated by the allegedly bookish, self-absorbed, and timid literary culture of the day.

A major component of Sacher-Masoch's success in this respect is his portrayal of Demetrius through the character's own language, an often unpolished and unliterary idiom that in its hesitations, clichés, and reliance on a small number of frequently repeated stock phrases represents a technique that anticipates some of the aesthetic aims of the Naturalists late in the century. The deficiencies in Demetrius' use of language also invite the reader to engage in a critical evaluation of the merits of Demetrius' arguments by revealing the searching, but sometimes shallow and self-serving mind at work behind them.

At first glance, "Der Capitulant" is a more conventional tale of unhappy love: two young Ruthenian peasants, Katharina and Frinko, fall in love, but she attracts the eye of the local nobleman, and eventually becomes mistress of his great estate, causing Frinko to join the army. The unusual aspect of the tale is the attempt on the part of Frinko and the other peasants in the tale to understand the economic necessity that underlay Katharina's decision. Kolanko, who is said to be over a hundred years old, articulates the story's point most clearly: "A woman has to eke out an existence just like a man, but how should she do it? . . . Nature hasn't given her any stamina, and she hasn't learned anything worthwhile, no trade or anything, so of course she tries to live off a man or uses him to make her fortune. Look at all a man has to do to climb up in the world, while a pretty young thing just has to show her face, or sometimes a little more, and suddenly she's changed from a milkmaid to a grand lady"(111). While such insight suffices to allow Frinko to maintain a pure-hearted love for Katharina, it leads him to the startling conclusion that, while a man can love romantically, with his whole heart, a woman's position precludes her from doing so.

Katharina is in some ways typical of Sacher-Masoch's female characters: her predatory eroticism does not result from distorted biological theories or philosophical mysogynism, but from the author's belief that women, a disadvantaged, even oppressed sex, have only their erotic domination over men to achieve the advantages that men realize by other means, such as birth, education, or economic independence.

"Mondnacht," the third Novelle, is the story of Olga, the wife of a Ruthenian estate owner, Mihael, who forces her to live in isolation from the larger world of the district capital and who loses interest in her as he becomes involved in the district's political life. Olga resolves to take a lover, Vladimir, in order to make her husband jealous. Vladimir, a gifted, hard-working man, is originally contemptuous of this frivolous and spoiled creature, but they eventually fall passionately in love with each other. After a year in which Olga shares Vladimir's life and assimilates his view, their affair is discovered, and her husband kills Vladimir in a duel. Olga, who remains with Mihael for the sake of their children and because of her need to be loved, becomes a somnambulist driven to tell her story to the narrator (who is identified as "Leopold"). She says that her only sin is "that she was raised like women are raised, to give pleasure, not to work like a man" (128).

A strikingly unpleasant aspect of the stories is the crude stereotyping and rude treatment to which the Jewish tavern keeper and his wife ("Don Juan") and the Jewish coachman ("Moonlight") are subjected. This insensitivity is the more egregious by virtue of Sacher-Masoch's later reputation among the Jews of central and eastern Europe as a friend and protector who used his fiction as a weapon in the fight against the sharpening anti-Semitism of the last several decades of the ninteenth century.[11]

The tavern-keeper nods in a "ducklike" fashion, is "close-fisted" and has "green" skin, and his mouth has "mockingly twisted, sour corners." And his wife, whose soulful eyes the narrator compares to a "vampire out of the grave of a rotting human nature," is "unpleasantly sharp" in her features.

But in the very same paragraph in which he so demonizes the Jewish woman, he solicits his reader's understanding by offering an explanation for what he perceives as her corrupted nature: "Pain, humiliation, whippings, and kicks had burrowed their way into her people's features for so long that they took on this incandescently wilted, wistfully contemptuous, humbly vengeful expression" (20).

NOTES

1. Portions of the afterword previously appeared in O'Pecko, "Comedy and Didacticity in Leopold von Sacher-Masoch's 'Venus im Pelz,'" *Modern Austrian Literature*, 1992 (vol. 25, no. 2): 1-14.

2. *Westermann's Jahrbuch der Illustrirten Deutschen Monatshefte* October 1866: 1-26.

3. *Der Salon für Literatur, Kunst und Gesellschaft* 1868: 94-108, 155-174.

4. *Der Salon für Literatur, Kunst und Gesellschaft* 1868: 57-108.

5. *Deutsche Monatsblätter* (Bremen) II, 3 (June, 1879): 263-264, reprinted in Sacher-Masoch, *Souvenirs*, ed. Susanne Farin (Munich: edition belleville, 1985) 66-67.

6. Reprinted in Sacher-Masoch, *Don Juan von Kolomea: Galizische Geschichten*, ed. Michael Farin (Bonn: Bouvier, 1985), pp. 188-194.

7. "Prospekt des Werkes *Das Vermächtnis Kains*," sent by Sacher-Masoch to J. G. Cotta and reprinted in ibid., pp. 179-180. All translations are mine.

8. For a more thorough treatment of Schopenhauer's influence on German and Austrian literature of the period, see *Geschichte der deutschen Literatur vom 18. Jahrhundert bis zur Gegenwart*, Viktor megač (Königstein/Ts.: Athenäum, 1985), vol. II (1848-1918), pp. 16-17 and *Deutsche Literatur im bürgerlichen Realismus 1848-1898* by Fritz Martini (Stuttgart: J. B. Metzlersche Verlagsbuchhandlung, 1964²), pp. 35-37. My discussion of Schopenhauer's philosophy and its influence is based on these works.

9. "Wanderer," p. 14. All page numbers referring to "Don Juan," "Der Capitulant," and "Mondnacht" also refer to this edition.

10. In addition, Michael Farin believes that a number of the later *Novellen* can be ascribed to the uncompleted cycles (Sacher-Masoch, *Don Juan von Kolomea*, ed. Michael Farin, p. 184).

11. See the "Afterword" (pp. 329-336) in Sacher-Masoch's *A Light for Others and other Jewish Tales from Galicia*, trans. by Michael O'Pecko (Riverside, CA: Ariadne Press, 1994).

Other Titles
by
Leopold von Sacher-Masoch
published by
ARIADNE PRESS

*A Light for Others
and Other
Jewish Tales from Galicia*
Translated and with an Afterword
by Michael T. O'Pecko
Contents:
Foreword: Sacher-Masoch Remembered
by Carl Spitteler
The Jewish Sects in Galicia
The Red Pepperman's Evil Spirit
Hasara Raba
My Tailor Abrahamek
A Light for Others
Pintschev and Mintschev

ISBN 0-929497-93-7
1994

*Jewish Life
Tales from Nineteenth-Century Europe*
Translated and with an Afterword
by Virginia L. Lewis

ISBN 1-57241-114-7
2002

As a young writer, Leopold von Sacher-Masoch (1836-1895) planned an ambitious cycle of thirty-six novellas grouped around six themes (love, property, the state, war, work, and death). This cycle was intended to portray "all of mankind's great problems, all the dangers of existence, all of humanity's ills." Only the first volume, entitled *Love*, was completed as planned.
Three of *Love*'s six novellas, along with a prologue entitled "The Wanderer," are presented here. Like many progressive writers of the nineteenth century, Sacher-Masoch was intrigued by the variations of love that did not conform easily to the era's conventional portraits of married happiness and explored those themes in this collection. "Don Juan of Kolomea," who finds himself deprived of his wife's affections after the birth of their child, seeks out erotic liaisons with any desirable woman who might cross his path even while he recognizes their meaninglessness. "The Man Who Re-Enlisted," spurned by his peasant girl who chooses a rich husband over her own happiness, continues to love her from afar and develops a deep understanding of the unhappy choices poverty, class, and gender can force upon a woman. Finally, "Moonlight," portrays a woman who, her mind awakened by another man's intellectual ambitions and social idealism, betrays her husband but is doomed to continue living with him after he kills her lover in a duel.

Sacher-Masoch's work is notable for its psychological insight in a pre-Freudian era and for his ability to evoke the exoticism of the "Wild East" of the Habsburg empire's Slavic territories. Both strengths are vividly displayed in *Love*.

Michael T. O'Pecko is a Professor of German at Towson University in Maryland. He previously translated Sacher-Masoch's *A Light for Others and Other Jewish Tales from Galicia* for Ariadne Press.

ISBN 1-57241-119-8